Sadie Rose
AND THE
MYSTERIOUS STRANGER

A SADIE ROSE ADVENTURE

Sadie Rose
AND THE
MYSTERIOUS
STRANGER

Hilda Stahl

CROSSWAY BOOKS • WHEATON, ILLINOIS
A DIVISION OF GOOD NEWS PUBLISHERS

Sadie Rose and the Mysterious Stranger

Copyright © 1993 by Word Spinners, Inc.

Published by Crossway Books
           a division of Good News Publishers
           1300 Crescent St.
           Wheaton, Illinois 60187.

Cover illustration: Robert Spellman

Art Direction/Design: Mark Schramm

First printing, 1993

Printed in the United States of America

Library of Congress Cataloging-in-Publication Data
Stahl, Hilda.
   Sadie Rose and the Mysterious Stranger / Hilda Stahl.
      p.   cm. — (A Sadie Rose adventure; #11)
   Summary: Sadie and Opal learn to trust God as they find their way through an adventure at a Nebraska poor farm.
   [1. Frontier and pioneer life—Fiction.   2. Nebraska—Fiction.   3. Christian life—Fiction.]
I. Title.   II. Series: Stahl, Hilda. Sadie Rose adventure; bk. 11.
PZ7.S78244Saf   1993   [Fic]—dc20   93-4203
ISBN 0-89107-747-2

01	00	99	98	97	96	95	94	93
15	14	13	12	11	10	9	8	7	6	5	4	3	2	1

*Dedicated with love
to Sarah Stahl*

Contents

1

Opal's Gloves

Her feet braced against the wagon, Sadie lifted her face to the warm Nebraska wind and laughed happily. Her laughter floated out over the vast prairie and up into the bright blue April sky. Finally the long cold winter was over! She was sitting on one side of Caleb and Opal on the other, and they were heading east to Starr to get the lumber to build Momma's frame house. Momma had had enough of living in the two-room sod house, especially after mice had chewed her favorite spring bonnet into shreds and left tracks all over a pound of freshly churned butter that Helen had left uncovered on the table. Caleb had finally saved enough money by selling cattle and horses from the Circle Y to build the frame house.

Suddenly Opal gripped Caleb's arm, looked into

his face shaded by his wide-brimmed hat, and cried, "Daddy, you have to turn back!"

Alarmed, Sadie looked around Caleb at Opal. Had Opal decided to stay home after all? Opal had said she wanted to go with them just because she never got to do anything except stay home and work or go to school.

Caleb pulled on the reins to make Dick and Jane slow down but not stop. "What's wrong, Opal?" he asked in his soft Texas drawl. He'd been a cowboy in Texas for years, then had driven a herd of cattle up to Nebraska for the good grass, and had decided to stay.

"I forgot my gloves!" At fifteen going on sixteen, things like that were important to Opal.

Sadie rolled her eyes. "Who cares about gloves!" Sadie was thirteen, and she didn't like wearing gloves or a bonnet, even if Momma said ladies wore both. Momma had been born and raised in Michigan, and she knew what ladies did and didn't do. She said that just because they lived in the wild frontier, they wouldn't be wild, but would have manners and schooling.

Caleb slowed the team down even more. "Opal, are you sure you need your gloves?"

Opal looked ready to burst into tears. She blinked her wide blue eyes, and her lips trembled. "Daddy, I can't be seen in public without them! What would people think?"

Sadie looked back over her shoulder toward home and groaned. They really weren't that far away from home, but she hated to waste even a minute. She'd never been to Starr before. She'd been to Jake's Crossing, the town nearest the Circle Y, and she'd been to Vida. It had stores and houses made of lumber instead of sod like at Jake's Crossing.

Caleb had said Starr was bigger than both towns put together. It was going to be frighteningly exciting to go there.

Caleb smiled at Opal, then turned Dick and Jane back toward the ranchhouse. They were still on Circle Y property since it took close to an hour to get off Circle Y land.

Retying her calico bonnet back on so Momma wouldn't scold, Sadie watched ten-year-old Web and nine-year-old Helen stop picking up dried cow chips they used for fuel and turn toward the wagon. Tanner barked and streaked across the new spring grass toward the wagon. Momma stepped out of the sod house and shielded her eyes against the bright sun to see why Tanner was barking. Riley, who at seventeen years was as big as a man and worked as hard as one, hurried out of the barn and looked too. Sadie looked for Adabelle Hepford, the Missouri woman who was staying in the small sod house. Then Sadie remembered that Adabelle had gone yesterday to stay with the old pioneer woman Jewel Ferguson so she could learn more about the ways of the prairie. Adabelle was going to marry Judge Loggia soon. They were going to build a house and live on their own homestead. Adabelle had to learn how to survive that kind of life.

Brushing back strands of nutmeg-brown hair, Opal flushed with embarrassment at the family watching them return. When she'd put her white gloves on this morning, she'd discovered a terrible hole in the finger of her left glove. She'd quickly mended it with tiny stitches, then left the gloves on the bed while she put away Momma's sewing basket. Sadie had made her hurry so much that she'd forgotten to pick them up again.

Sadie wanted to scowl at Opal, but she knew Jesus didn't want her to be mean.

Caleb stopped the team near the well, and Opal jumped to the ground and ran to the sod house.

Momma rubbed her hands down her flowered apron that almost covered her short, plump body and hurried toward the wagon. "What's wrong?"

"Not a thing, Bess!" Caleb dropped to the ground and hugged Momma as if he hadn't kissed her good-bye just a few minutes earlier.

Sadie flushed and looked quickly away. Caleb had married Momma a year ago after Pa had died in the blizzard. Then Caleb moved the family from Douglas County clear across Nebraska to his ranch at the edge of the sandhills. Pa had never kissed Momma when anyone was watching, but Caleb kissed her anytime he pleased. Momma blushed when he did, but she never pushed him away. She liked his hugs and kisses.

With her blonde-white braids flipping on her thin shoulders, Helen skidded to a stop beside the wagon with Web next to her just as Riley walked up.

"How come you came back, Sadie?" Helen asked. She wished Caleb was returning so she and Web could go along.

"Opal forgot her gloves." Sadie rolled her eyes.

Riley laughed and shook his head. "I thought it was something more important."

"Like Daddy forgetting the cash money for the lumber," Web said with a grin. But he knew that wasn't possible. He'd handed Caleb the leather money belt right after breakfast.

Opal ran out of the sod house, tugging her gloves on. "I'm sorry, Daddy, but I just had to have them."

"I know." Caleb hugged Opal close, then helped her climb up and sit on the wagon seat.

Momma reached up and patted Opal's leg. "I wish you had new gloves."

Opal smiled. "I'll keep the finger hidden, and no one will know they aren't new." She held up the finger she'd carefully mended, then turned her hand so no one could see it. "It'll be just fine."

"We're all pleased about that," Caleb said with a grin. He winked at the kids, and they giggled. They all knew how Opal was.

Caleb kissed Momma one more time, then climbed into place between Opal and Sadie. "See you all late tomorrow night or maybe the night after. Take care, and don't worry about us."

"We won't," Momma said, standing with her head high. Momma very seldom cried, even though she wanted to. Sending the girls and Caleb off across the prairie to Starr was a hard thing to do. "We'll be praying the lumber will be waiting . . . and for your safe return."

Sadie smiled and lifted her hand in a wave as Caleb slapped the reins on Dick and Jane and called for them to get moving.

"Bring me a candy stick!" Helen shouted.

"I will," Caleb called back.

Sadie frowned. Helen was very spoiled. She knew better than to ask for a candy stick when all their cash money was going to pay for the lumber for the new house.

"Have fun!" Riley called as he waved. He'd wanted to go with them, but he had to take care of the cattle, fix a fence, and start training a horse Caleb had just bought.

"We'll have fun," Opal shouted back, then laughed happily. They would have fun! She might

13

even meet a fine young man. She flushed and wanted to grab the thought back. El Hepford was her fine young man, and they'd even talked about getting married when she turned sixteen in June. She lifted her chin, faced the bright sun, and let the warm breeze blow against her face. She *was* going to have fun!

Sadie moved restlessly on the seat as she thought about the long trip ahead. Maybe Caleb would tell one of his tall tales about when he was a cowboy in Texas.

Caleb suddenly laughed. "You gals want to hear about the time I met Pecos Bill?"

Sadie grinned and settled back to listen to Caleb. The next three hours flew by. When Pa was alive, he'd never said more than a couple of words a day. Caleb had more words in him than anyone Sadie had ever met—unless it was Mitch Hepford. He could talk all day without stopping!

Just as the team rounded a low hill, a shot rang out. Opal and Sadie screamed and ducked. Caleb reached for the Colt .45 on his left hip, but before he could draw, another shot rang out.

"Get your hands up, mister! And don't try for your gun again!" A man on a roan rode into sight, holding a rifle aimed right at Caleb. The man was about Caleb's age and looked like a homesteader in faded overalls, blue workshirt, and a battered-looking cap instead of a wide-brimmed hat. "Stop the team, and put your hands up!"

"Daddy, what shall we do?" Opal whispered.

"Stay calm and quiet, girls."

Sadie longed to use the rifle in the scabbard beside her. She could shoot the wings off a fly, but being as good as Annie Oakley didn't help a bit in the tight spot they were in. Was the man after Caleb's

14

money belt? But how could he be? It didn't show, and nobody could know he had it.

Caleb pulled back on the reins and shouted, "Whoa, Dick! Whoa, Jane!"

The team stopped, and the sudden silence made Sadie shiver. She stared at the homesteader and waited for him to speak. He stared right back at her, then stared at Opal. Sadie trembled. What was wrong with him?

With a moan he lowered his rifle. "Sorry, folks. You ain't who I thought you were."

Sadie felt the tension ooze out of Caleb.

"I'm Caleb York of the Circle Y, and these are my girls, Sadie and Opal. I reckon you better be more careful with that rifle of yours."

"I know." The man rubbed an unsteady hand across his eyes and cleared his throat. "I've been looking for my two girls for three days now. They're about the size of your girls."

Caleb looped the reins around the brake handle and dropped to the ground. "You look about done in. We got food in the back of the wagon."

The man slid off his horse and leaned weakly against it. "I don't know as I could eat."

Sadie and Opal slid close to each other and clung together.

"Can I be of help?" Caleb asked softly.

"I don't guess anybody can be." The man finally lifted his head. "I'm Scott Elston. We live west of Starr on a new homestead. I went to Starr a few days ago with my wife and girls. The girls are big—the size of your girls—not babies, so I said they could walk around town on their own. They wanted to look at everything." Scott Elston rubbed his eyes again. "Victoria and Clarissa." He grinned a crooked grin. "The wife wanted grand names for 'em." He swallowed hard. "They don't get to town much. I let them walk around, but . . . they disappeared." He flung out his arm helplessly and let it drop to his side. "Just disappeared. I took Ruth home to tend the chores, and I set out to look for 'em."

Caleb pushed his hat to the back of his head. He knew how he'd feel if his girls disappeared. "Is there law in Starr?"

Scott shook his head. "The man at the general store said a marshall rides through once, maybe twice a year."

"Sorry to hear that." Caleb looped his thumbs in his gunbelt and stood with his booted feet apart. "Didn't anyone in town see your girls?"

"Sure, but nobody saw 'em walk away from town or get carried away by anybody. The wife thought maybe Indians done it, but there wasn't no Indians around that would do such a terrible thing."

Opal clung tightly to Sadie. What would she do if something terrible happened to her and Sadie?

Sadie shivered. What had happened to Victoria and Clarissa Elston?

2

Horace Wippet

In Starr, Sadie sat in the wagon with Opal while Caleb walked across the sandy lumberyard to the office. In his high slant-heeled boots Caleb looked more at home on the back of a horse than he did walking. The screen door squawked as he opened it. The noise of all the buggies, wagons, and horses along with people shouting back and forth and kids running wildly down the dusty street pressed against Sadie, and she wanted to cover her ears with her hands. One of the things she liked most about the prairie was the great silence. Opal nervously pushed her nutmeg-brown hair over her shoulder, and then she brushed dust off her calico dress and retied her matching bonnet. "Daddy said we could get out and walk around," Opal said in a low voice as if she were afraid someone would hear her.

"I know." Sadie swallowed hard. Was she such a coward that she couldn't walk among a large crowd of people without being frightened? Sadie tugged her bonnet off and let the warm wind blow against her head. Brown braids hung over her thin shoulders onto her calico dress. She wished she could've worn her cowboy hat, but Momma wouldn't hear of letting her wear it to town. Sadie sighed as she looked at the stacks of lumber in neat rows, then the wagons lining the hitchrails. "I don't know if I want to walk around."

"Nothing will happen to us." Shivering, Opal's face blanched. "Nothing like what happened to those poor girls Victoria and Clarissa Elston will happen to us."

"I know," Sadie said again. But what if it did?

Scott Elston had eaten a fried chicken leg and a biscuit while he stood with Caleb at the back of the wagon. He'd looked right at Sadie and said, "My girls have dark hair and eyes much like yours. I'm going home to see if the girls are there, but if they aren't, I'll go out again. I'll never give up looking for them!" He'd sounded hopeless. Sadie felt sad just thinking about Victoria and Clarissa.

Her face set with determination, Opal jumped up. "I am going to walk to the store and look at ladies' hats!" She'd seen them as they drove through town to get to the lumberyard and had declared then and there she would look at them—she'd even dare to try one on.

Sadie sighed. She didn't want to stay in the wagon either, but she sure didn't want to look at hats.

Lifting her skirts carefully, Opal climbed over the wagon and started down the wheel. Suddenly her toe caught, and she started to fall. She screamed, but her scream was cut short when someone caught her and held her in strong arms.

Sadie sank back on the seat as she watched the man look at Opal the same way all boys and men looked at her—as if she were the most beautiful creature alive.

Opal looked into the man's face, and her heart stood still. He had eyes as blue as hers and hair the color of ripe wheat. He was over twenty and stronger than Caleb. She didn't want him to put her down, yet she knew she had to ask him to. She smiled and whispered, "Please, put me down."

He smiled and didn't make a move to lower her to the ground. He was shorter than Caleb and had a broad chest and arms as big around as Helen's whole body. "I'm mighty glad I was here in time to catch you." His voice was as deep as Riley's and had a slight accent, similar to Mary Ferguson's from England.

"Me, too. Thank you." Opal felt weak all over, and she made no move to leave the security of his strong arms. "I'm Opal York."

Sadie impatiently twisted the strings of her bonnet.

The man bowed his head slightly. "Michael Treet. Call me Mike."

Sadie bit back a crabby remark.

Opal smiled. "Mike." Just saying his name sent chills over her.

"I sure don't want to leave you, but I'm meeting a man inside the office. I hope you don't vanish into thin air just after you came into my lonely life." He reluctantly placed her on the ground.

Opal touched his strong forearm. "Thank you again."

He squeezed her gloved hand, then hurried to

the door. He turned and winked at her, then walked inside.

Opal leaned weakly against the wagon.

Scowling, Sadie dropped to the ground. "How dare he wink at you! What's wrong with you, Opal?"

"He's just like the prince in a fairy tale!"

"And you're the poor, raggedy servant girl who wins his heart," Sadie said with a laugh.

Opal gasped and stared down at her glove. "He saw the mending on my glove! I know he did! What'll I do? I'm so embarrassed."

Sadie jabbed Opal's arm. "Have you forgotten about Ellis Hepford?"

Opal gasped. She had forgotten about him! "Don't be ridiculous! Besides, I probably will never see Michael Treet again." She sighed. "Mike," she whispered. The sound of his name on her lips made her tingle all over.

"Then it doesn't matter that he saw your mended glove."

Opal hid her hand behind her back. "I should've left them home! Oh, why can't I have a beautiful new pair of gloves?"

Sadie leaned close to Opal. "Because our money is going toward Momma's new house."

Opal frowned. "I know that!" She patted her cheeks and took a deep breath. "Let's go look at the hats."

"If we must." Sadie walked down the wooden sidewalk as she thought about the saddle she'd seen in the window of the saddle shop. She wanted to price a saddle for Apple's foal to be born yet this month—maybe while they were gone! She'd told Web and Helen to keep a close watch on Apple. Sadie knew they would.

At the store with the hats in the window, Opal

gaped at the hats as she held her hand on her throat. They were all so beautiful they took her breath away, but one in particular stood out. She nudged Sadie and pointed, too excited to remember how unladylike it was to point. "Look, Sadie! It is the most beautiful hat I've ever seen!" It was a wide-brimmed, white straw hat with a huge red scarf wrapped around it as a band. The scarf streamed down the back of the hat, and huge paper roses cov-ered the front with a huge, white, soft feather at the side. "I want that hat, Sadie!"

"It is pretty," Sadie admitted reluctantly. The more she studied it, the prettier it became. She wanted that hat for herself! Never had she thought she'd want anything so badly. It was as strong of a want as when she'd wanted the black cowboy hat. The saddle shop floated right out of her head. She wanted to put the hat on her head and see herself in the looking glass. In that hat she might look as beau-tiful as Opal!

Suddenly Opal burst into tears. She turned away from the people walking toward them and tried to hide her tears from them.

"What's wrong?" Sadie whispered in alarm. Opal didn't cry often.

"I get tired of never getting what I want! I want that hat! Why can't I get it? Why?"

Sadie gently patted Opal's back. "You know why. We don't have cash money."

"Then I'll trade for it!"

"What can you trade? You don't have anything."

"I know." Opal turned to walk away and bumped right into a man. She looked into his face and fell back from him. He was as young and handsome as a prince in a fairy tale, but his eyes were ice-blue. He was only a couple of inches taller than she was and very strong. He smiled at her as she pulled away.

A chill ran down Sadie's spine, but she didn't know why.

"Pardon me, miss," the man said.

"My fault. Please forgive me." Opal stepped closer to Sadie.

He doffed his hat, revealing hair as dark as Opal's. "I haven't seen you girls in town before."

Opal couldn't find her voice. Sadie didn't want to talk to the man, so she kept her lips sealed.

He smiled, and his eyes softened. "Horace Wippet at your service, ladies. Welcome to Starr. It's a fine town."

Opal remembered all of Momma's teachings on being a polite lady, and she managed to say with a smile, "I'm Opal, and this is my sister Sadie. We were admiring the hats, but we don't have any money to buy one." Oh, why had she said that!

"That's too bad. Maybe you can get the price of a hat from your parents."

"We can't," Sadie said quickly. She tugged Opal's arm. "We have to go."

"Is your family looking for you?" Horace Wippet asked as he glanced quickly around the busy street.

Opal excused herself and hurried away with Sadie. They didn't stop until they reached the general store. "I didn't like that man," Opal whispered.

"Me either." Sadie walked into the general store first and gasped at the variety of items. A bald-headed clerk wearing a big white apron was adding up a customer's bill as she chattered on about the warm spring weather. Sadie blocked out the woman's voice as she walked slowly down an aisle. The store was much bigger than the one in Vida and had a whole rack of ready-made dresses and shirt-waists and skirts, as well as men's clothing. Bolts of fabric were lined up on two long shelves. She touched a red silk and breathed in the smell of the new material. In a daze she walked through the store with Opal following her oohing and ahhhing over everything— even the stovepipes and hammers and nails. Just as they reached the cracker barrel Horace Wippet walked in. They ducked quickly out of sight behind the shelf that held canned goods so they wouldn't have to speak to him again. They peeked between cans of peaches to watch him.

"Hello, Horace!" the clerk said with pleasure. "I'm glad to see you."

"Horace!" the woman customer said excitedly. "It's always a delight to see you."

Horace took off his hat and held it in his hands. His brown hair was parted in the middle and combed neatly. He looked younger without his hat, almost as young as Riley. He smiled. "Thank you, Mrs. Bosley. Give your family my regards."

"I surely will. We'll see you in church on Sunday."

"You can count on it."

After Mrs. Bosley walked out, the clerk said, "How's it going at the farm?"

"Very well, thank you. I trust your business is doing well."

"Best week yet!"

"I'm pleased to hear that."

Opal and Sadie looked at each other. "We were wrong about him," Sadie whispered, and Opal nodded.

Smiling, the clerk clamped a hand on Horace's shoulder. "I have a box of things for you to take to the kids at The Poor Farm."

"That's kind of you."

Opal and Sadie stayed out of Horace Wippet's sight, but listened to the conversation. After Horace left, the girls walked up to the clerk.

The clerk beamed at them. "You should've met the man who was just in here. He's wonderful and has helped the community and the kids in it. Best thing ever to happen to Starr!"

"He seemed nice," Opal said in a small voice.

"'Nice' is an understatement. He's the director of The Poor Farm outside of town. He's young—not yet thirty years old, but he's done more than any other man in Starr for the orphans and poor folks."

"That's nice." Sadie didn't know what else to say.

The clerk nodded. "'Nice' is an understatement!" The clerk talked on and on until another customer attracted his attention.

The girls said a quick good-bye and hurried outdoors, then slowly walked down the sidewalk to the store with the hats. "I sure do want it," Opal said, and Sadie agreed.

While they stood there Horace Wippet walked up and tipped his hat. "We meet again, girls."

They smiled at him without hesitation.

He motioned to the hats. "I see you're looking at the hats again."

"Yes. But we still can't buy one," Opal said before she realized she was going to say it.

Horace pursed his lips and looked thoughtful, then smiled. "Maybe I can help."

Sadie cocked her head. She was ready to hear any suggestion he could make. "How?"

Horace looked from Opal to Sadie, then back to Opal. "I know someone who'll hire you to work and will pay you well for it."

"You do?" Opal's pulse leaped. Maybe there was a way to buy the hat!

"Where would we work, and what would we do?" Sadie asked, trying not to sound too excited, but failing.

"The job is just outside of town, and you'd work for me."

Opal locked her gloved fingers together. "Doing what?"

"I have a variety of jobs you could do. You could go with me now to see what I have available and decide if you want to work. You're free to come right back or to work as long or as short as you want. I'd pay you according to how well and how fast you work. You could easily make enough to buy the hat."

"I'm willing," Opal said.

Sadie frowned thoughtfully. "How would we get there?"

"You could walk, but you're welcome to ride with me. I have my wagon. I picked up supplies, and now I'm ready to go." Horace squared his shoulders. "If you're hesitant about going with me, ask anybody about me. They'll all vouch for me."

"We'll go," Opal said quickly.

Horace looked at Sadie. "How about you, little brown eyes?"

Sadie giggled. "I'll go. I might be small for my age, but I can work hard. I know a lot about hard work. Don't I, Opal?"

"We both do. And we don't mind working."

"Good. Then come with me. I'll bring you back whenever you say, or you can walk back. It'll be up to you."

Sadie hesitated. Should they tell Caleb where they were going? He'd said they were on their own, so it wouldn't really matter. They'd be back in town before dark and tell him their exciting news. Pictures of how she'd look in the beautiful hat made her pulse leap. She followed Opal and Horace to his wagon and climbed in. They were on the way to The Poor Farm to work to make enough money to buy the hat. How surprised Caleb would be when he learned they'd made themselves so useful!

Sadie looked toward the lumberyard so she could wave at Caleb if he was in sight. He wasn't. Just then a black cowboy wearing a huge white hat and riding a white horse caught her attention. He was a Negro, but something about him looked like Caleb. Maybe it was the way he sat in the saddle, or maybe it was the coiled whip he carried over his shoulder just like Caleb often did.

The man caught Sadie's eye and smiled. She lifted her hand in a wave and smiled back. Folks in Starr were nice! First Horace Wippet, and now the black cowboy.

Sadie settled down in the back of the wagon next to the supplies and smiled happily.

The Poor Farm

Sadie climbed slowly from the wagon as she looked around at The Poor Farm. It looked like a regular farm with a few barns and a huge garden area where several children were working, but the house was different. It was a long, gray, one-story frame building with very few windows and a brick chimney at each end. Horses and cattle grazed in a pasture surrounded by a barbed-wire fence. A windmill stood next to one of the barns. Its blades whirring in the warm wind was the only sound to be heard. Sadie frowned. Why weren't the children laughing and talking as they worked? Why didn't they run to see who'd just arrived?

Horace jumped to the ground. The horses moved restlessly, jangling their harness. "I'll get somebody to unload the supplies, and then I'll take you to the glove factory to show you that first."

Flushing, Opal thought of her mended glove and quickly hid that finger. On the way from Starr, Horace had told her about the glove factory where many orphaned children and adults without homes worked. She longed for a pair of new gloves, and then she wouldn't have to be embarrassed if she fell into Mike's arms again.

With an iron bar Horace struck a bronze bell that hung on a wooden arm at the side of the house. Instantly a boy ran to the wagon and without a greeting or a smile picked up a box and carried it inside.

Sadie picked up another box and started to follow the boy, but Horace stopped her.

"Josh will do it. He knows right where everything goes." Horace motioned for Sadie to put the box back.

She hesitated, then obeyed. Josh rushed out again, and she smiled and said, "Hi." He didn't even look at her or speak to her. That made her feel strange. She glanced at Opal to see her reaction, but Opal was too engrossed in something Horace was saying about the glove factory.

When Josh finished unloading the supplies, Horace struck the the bell again, twice this time. A boy older than Josh ran out of the barn without a word or a look at anyone and led the team to the barn.

Horace smiled and gallantly took Opal's arm. "Now, we'll look at the glove factory to see what you girls would like to do."

Just then Sadie spotted a boy working with a black horse in a corral. "I'm good with horses," Sadie said as she hurried along with Horace and Opal. "I could help the boy in the corral."

Horace stopped and looked toward the corral. "Rann does seem to be having a problem. But he's not used to having a girl help him. He wouldn't be polite at all."

"I don't mind. I could settle the horse down and get the bridle on without any trouble. He must have a tender mouth. The boy is too rough. Some horses with tender mouths need a gentle touch."

Horace frowned thoughtfully and finally nodded. "If it makes you happy to work with the horse, then do it. Tell Rann I sent you. But don't be surprised when he doesn't speak to you."

Sadie smiled and lifted her chin proudly. She'd show Horace just what a good worker she was! Maybe she could even teach Rann a thing or two about horses. She'd learned a lot from Caleb in the last year.

As Horace and Opal walked to the building that looked like a large chicken house with windows, Sadie ran toward the corral. Dust puffed onto her hightop shoes. Her skirt hung well below her knees. Momma had said that this year when they made new clothes for her, they'd make them long. Sometimes she was excited about wearing long dresses, other times not.

Several feet from the corral Sadie slowed to a walk. She didn't want to spook the horse or make Rann angry. She carefully opened the wooden gate just wide enough to slip through, then closed it again. Rann never said a word or even looked her way. He was about her age with shaggy, light brown hair and a pinched look about his wide mouth.

"Horace said I was to help you," Sadie said.

Rann looked at her, then went right back to trying to force the bit between the horse's teeth. Dust filled the air as the horse danced away from Rann.

Sadie walked to Rann's side. "Let me try."

Rann pushed the bridle into her hands, then

29

just stood there. His ragged and dusty clothes hung on his thin frame. She hadn't noticed before that he was barefoot.

Sadie held the bridle in one hand and touched the horse with the other. "What's his name?"

Rann didn't answer.

Sadie looked at Rann sharply. Wasn't he able to talk? "Horace said I was to help you. So, let's work together like he wants."

Rann gripped the horse's rope halter.

Sadie looked closer at Rann. "Can't you talk?"

He nodded.

"Then talk to me! Horace said I was to help you."

"Did he say I could talk?"

"Of course!" Sadie frowned. Horace actually hadn't said Rann could talk, but he hadn't said he shouldn't. "What's the horse's name?"

"I call him Soot because he's black."

Sadie smiled at Rann. "Good name. You hold the bridle a while so I can talk to Soot and calm him down."

Rann took the bridle and let Sadie hold Soot by the halter. Rann twisted his toe in the dust. "Did Mr. Wippet say you could call him Horace?"

"Yes." Sadie gently patted Soot's neck as she looked at Rann.

Rann shivered. "Don't you got no folks?"

"Sure, I do! My sister Opal is looking at the glove factory. Caleb York, my daddy, is in Starr. The rest of the family is home on the Circle Y Ranch."

Rann brushed his hair out of his gray eyes. "How come Mr. Wippet brought you here then?"

"So we could work and make enough money to buy a hat."

Rann frowned. "He don't pay nobody to work here. He won't pay you either."

Sadie didn't understand why Rann was saying such a thing. But maybe Rann was an orphan, and maybe orphans didn't get paid because they worked for their keep. She turned to Soot and talked to him soothingly. Finally she took the bridle from Rann and gently, slowly eased the bit into Soot's mouth, then slipped the bridle up over his ears and buckled it at the side of his jaw. "There."

Rann smiled. "Why'd he let you do that?"

She told him, then added, "When you rein him while you're riding him, do it gently to keep from hurting his mouth. Now what are we supposed to do?"

"Saddle him."

"You sure? Has he had one on before?"

"No."

"Then just put the blanket on and let him get used to that."

Rann frowned. "Mr. Wippet expects me to be riding Soot before the day is out. I can't eat or go to bed until I do."

"That's crazy!"

Rann gasped and darted a look toward the glove factory. "Don't you never say that where Mr. Wippet can hear you or he'll beat you and make you go without food for three days."

"Rann! That's a terrible thing to say about Horace!"

"Maybe so, but it's true." Rann rubbed the blanket against Soot, then carefully laid it on his back. He let it stay.

"Did he ever . . . beat you or make you . . . go without food?"

"Yes. The first year I was here."

Sadie felt sick to her stomach. She wondered if

31

she could believe Rann. "How long have you been here?"

"Three years."

"Three years! How old are you?"

"Thirteen."

"Are you an orphan?"

"No." Rann shook his head.

Sadie couldn't understand that at all. "Then why are you here?"

"I can't talk about it."

"Why not?"

Rann's eyes flashed with sudden anger, but then the anger faded, and his eyes were full of such hopelessness that Sadie almost cried out. "Mr. Wippet won't let me go. I ran away twice already, and he caught me and locked me up so I would know not to try again."

Sadie couldn't speak for a long time. "Why don't your folks come get you?"

"They don't know I'm here."

"Mr. Wippet could tell them," Sadie said. She didn't realize she was now calling the man Mr. Wippet rather than Horace.

"He won't. He told them I ran off and that he hasn't seen me since. They finally gave up coming here."

Sadie's head spun. "I'll tell your folks you're here. Where do they live?"

"Between Starr and Brewster on a homestead." Rann laid his arm across Soot's back. "It won't do no good to tell 'em. When they come, Mr. Wippet will lie to 'em, and they'll just leave again."

"But I'll tell them the truth!"

Rann shook his head. "Mr. Wippet won't let you. He won't even let you leave here."

Sadie's blood froze. "He can't stop us," she said in a weak voice.

"He'll stop you. He'll lock you up like he done them girls he brought here a few days ago."

Sadie's legs almost gave way. "What girls?"

"Two girls about your sister's size—color of hair like yours. They got real strange names I never heard before."

"Victoria and Clarissa Elston?" Sadie asked weakly.

Rann nodded.

"Where are they?"

"Locked in a room in the house until they obey Mr. Wippet without a fight and until their pa stops looking for 'em."

Sadie glanced toward the house. "Could I get inside and get them out?"

"You? You're a kid."

"I know, but I'm strong and I'm smart."

Rann eased the saddle onto Soot but didn't pull the cinch strap across. Soot let the saddle stay on. Rann turned back to Sadie. "Don't matter how smart or strong you are—Mr. Wippet is smarter and stronger."

Sadie leaned close to Rann. "He said we could leave anytime we wanted. I'm getting Opal, and I'm leaving right now!"

"He won't let you go."

Sadie's eyes flashed. "He can't keep me here! You'll see!"

"When he gives you a glass of water or lemonade to drink, don't drink it."

"Why?"

"It's got something in it that knocks you out. I seen him do it lots of times."

33

"How many kids are here that want to get away?"

Rann shrugged. "Lots of 'em."

"Why can't you figure out a plan and escape together?"

"We ain't allowed to talk to each other. Only reason I can talk to you is because Mr. Wippet told you I could talk."

Sadie thought back to exactly what Mr. Wippet had said, and she trembled. "Rann, he said to tell you I was to help you. He didn't say anything about you and me talking."

Rann sank against Soot. "If he sees me talking to you, he'll beat me."

"I'm sorry!" She wrung her hands. "I've got to do something to help you! Why can't you jump on Soot and ride to Starr? You could find my daddy and tell him your story. He'd help you."

Rann looked past Sadie, and the color drained from his face. "Here he comes. I can't say another word to you. And don't you try to make me!"

"I won't." Sadie led Soot around in a circle, then held the bridle strap as Rann looped the cinch strap loosely under Soot's belly.

"Sadie, come here," Horace called as he and Opal stopped near the corral.

"I'll help you, Rann," Sadie whispered. He didn't answer, but did barely nod. She ran to the gate and slipped through. "We got the bridle and saddle on."

"Good work." Horace smiled at Sadie. "But it's hot work. Come inside for a glass of lemonade."

Sadie's stomach knotted.

"I told Horace we should get back to town," Opal said. "We really should've told Daddy where we were going. I don't know what we were thinking!"

"You're right, Opal." Sadie moved close to Opal's

34

side. "We better get back to Starr where we belong."
And then they'd come back and set Rann, Victoria,
and Clarissa free!

Horace frowned. "I can't take the time to give
you a ride at this moment, but if you wait a while I'll
be free."

"We'll walk." Sadie caught Opal's hand. "We
don't mind, do we?"

Opal frowned. She *did* mind. It was too warm,
and she didn't know the way. They could easily get
turned around and walk out into the sandhills never
to be seen again. "A few more minutes won't matter
a bit."

Sadie lifted her chin. "Opal, I want to go *now*.
We can come back after we talk to Daddy." She managed to smile at Horace. "Our daddy is buying lumber in Starr. He'll wonder where we are if we don't get
right back, so we'll walk."

Horace shrugged. "Do as you want." He started
toward the house, then stopped and turned back.
"But come in for a drink first. It's a warm day, and
it's two miles to town. You need a nice cold drink."

Sadie forced back a shiver.

"I *am* thirsty," Opal said.

"We don't want a drink," Sadie said. She tugged
on Opal's arm. She had to get Opal away before she
drank the drink that would knock her out! "Let's go.
We'll get a drink in town."

Opal sighed. "All right." She couldn't understand why Sadie wanted to leave so desperately.

Sadie wanted to laugh with relief, but she didn't
flicker an eyelash.

Opal smiled at Horace. "I'm sorry it didn't work
out like we thought. We could never work long
enough to earn enough money for the hat."

"I'm sorry, too." Horace tipped his hat to them

and started for the house again. Again he stopped. "I can't let you go when I know you're thirsty. I'll bring water to you for a quick drink, then you can go."

"Thank you!" Opal moistened her dry lips. "I am mighty thirsty."

Sadie's heart sank. She had to keep Opal from drinking the water, but how?

4
Locked In

Sadie waited until Horace reached the door of the house, then whispered, "Don't drink what he gives you. Mr. Wippet is a wicked man!"

Opal frowned at Sadie. "Stop teasing me!"

Sadie's heart sank. "I'm not teasing! Please, please, believe me, Opal. We're in real danger!"

Opal laughed and jabbed Sadie's arms. "You can't make me fall for this. You and Riley are always trying to fool me just so you can laugh."

"Not this time!" Sadie grabbed Opal's arm. "Let's go right now! We can't wait for Mr. Wippet!"

Frowning, Opal pulled free. "Stop it! I'm going to tell Horace what you said."

Sadie gasped and shook her head hard. "No! I mean it, Opal!"

Just then Horace walked out of the house with two glasses of water. "Here you are, girls. Drink up, and then I'll drive you to town. I find I do have time after all."

Opal glanced at Sadie as if to say, "I told you so." She took the glass from Horace and immediately started drinking.

"Here, Sadie." Horace held the glass out to her, and she finally took it.

"Thank you," Sadie said weakly. How was she going to get out of drinking the water? She held the glass to her lips, but she didn't drink. Her head whirled as she tried to find an answer. Silently she cried out for God to help her.

Just then Soot whinnied and reared high. Horace turned to see what was going on. Sadie bent down and poured the water on the ground. With the side of her foot she spread dry sand over the wetness. Not even Opal had seen what she'd done.

Sadie's heart drummed so loudly, she was sure Horace must hear it. Now what would she do? She couldn't let Horace know she hadn't drunk the water. She'd have to watch Opal and do exactly what she did. Her mouth felt drier than sand. Her stomach fluttered wildly.

Rann calmed Soot, and Horace and Opal turned back. Opal's glass was empty, and she held it out to Horace with a thank you and a smile. Sadie did the same. Maybe Rann had been pulling her leg. Maybe the glass had been pure water—nothing more.

Just then Opal moaned and sank to the ground. Sadie cried out as she stared down at Opal. With all the courage in her, Sadie moaned and sank to the ground beside Opal.

Horace laughed wickedly. "You girls will be a big help to me around here. I'm glad you decided not to leave after all."

Sadie wanted to open her eyes and see what

38

was going on, but she kept them closed and stayed as quiet as she could. Soon someone picked her up as easily as picking up a baby. She smelled sweat and onions and felt a man's rough shirt.

"Take them to the room with the other two girls," Horace said sharply. "They'll sleep all night. If anyone comes looking for them, tell them no one's been here. I'll make sure Rann keeps quiet."

Sadie forced herself to stay limp and to keep her eyes shut. She could hear the screen door of the house open and felt the man carry her inside. She heard another person behind them and knew someone was carrying Opal. Footsteps sounded loud on the wood floor. Smells of frying potatoes and onions drifted after them. She heard a key grate in a lock and a door open. The man walked into a room and laid her on a bed. The room smelled closed in.

"Let us out of here!" a girl cried. It had to be either Victoria or Clarissa.

"Keep quiet unless you want to go without supper again tonight," the man barked.

Sadie lay very still. She heard the door close, and she heard sobbing.

"I want to go home," a girl said between sobs.

"I know, Rissa. I do too." The girl stood beside Sadie. "I wonder who they are. I wonder if they have a family or if they're orphans."

"Their clothes aren't new," Clarissa said. "See the patch on this girl's dress?"

Sadie had carefully sewed the patch on, but she knew if anyone looked close they'd see it. She had been glad to go without a new dress so Momma could have her house.

The girls stood beside the bed a long time talking. Finally they sank down onto the floor.

Sadie barely opened her eyes and peeked

through her lashes. The girls did indeed look similar to her and Opal! Their hair needed brushing, and
their faces were dirty. Sadie opened her eyes wider.
Dare she talk to the girls? She had to! "Girls . . ." she
whispered.

They gasped and stared at her in shock.

"Don't tell anyone, but I didn't drink the water
and didn't get knocked out like my sister did."

The girls scrambled to the edge of the bed. "Who
are you, and why'd you let them bring you in here?"

Sadie whispered her story. She didn't dare tell
them Rann was the one who'd helped or they might
accidentally let it out and cause him trouble. "When
will they unlock the door again?"

"For our supper, just before dark."

"Don't let on that I'm awake, please!"

"We won't," the girls said together.

Sadie lifted her head from the musty-smelling
mattress. "Do I dare get up?"

The girls nodded. "Nobody will come in here
until supper," the older girl said.

"Good." Sadie sat up, then looked at Opal
beside her. She looked as if she were sleeping com-
fortably and soundly. "How will she feel when she
wakes up?"

"Like she has cotton for a brain," one of the girls
said.

Her sister added, "Then she'll be real thirsty."

Sadie wanted to remember that so she would
know how to act if Caleb didn't find them by tonight.
Sadie pulled off Opal's gloves and tucked them in the
pocket of her petticoat. Finally she turned back to
the girls. "We met your pa on the road."

The girls cried out, then clamped their hands
over their mouths.

Sadie quickly told them about the meeting. "He says he won't give up looking for you."

Tears ran down their cheeks.

"Who's Victoria, and who's Clarissa?"

"I'm Victoria," the older girl said. "And she's Clarissa. I call her Rissa."

Clarissa rubbed tears off her face. "We plan to run away as soon as we're out of this room. Can you help us?"

"Yes!" Sadie looked very determined. "I am going to let the people in Starr know just how bad Horace Wippet is!"

Victoria hooked her tangled hair over her ears. "The woman who brings our meals says we won't get to be outdoors for a long time. She says we'll do jobs where nobody who comes here can spot us."

Sadie sat on the edge of the bed and thought about all Rann had told her and of what she'd seen of the layout of the farm. Somehow they'd have to convince Horace they had given up all hope of getting away. She told the girls what she'd decided. "We don't want him or any of his helpers to be suspicious of us and keep a sharp eye on us. When they aren't looking, we'll try to talk to the others. We'll find someone who wants to get away as badly as we do. If we can all work together, it'll make it easier."

"What if someone tells on us?" Clarissa asked with a shiver.

"We'll have to make sure we can trust the person before we say much."

They made plans on what they'd do in case Caleb didn't come looking for them that night. As they talked, Sadie heard footsteps outside the door. In a flash she laid back down and closed her eyes. She tried to breathe like Opal was breathing.

Victoria and Clarissa sat on the floor where

they'd been instructed to sit for meals. They both knew they were getting a bowl of bread and milk. They were each hungry enough to eat a whole chicken, a huge serving of fried potatoes, and a pan of biscuits.

The woman, who Sadie learned later was called Book because she loved to read, set the bowls in front of the girls, looked at Sadie and Opal, then walked out without a word. Horace forbade any of them to talk. If they did, they were whipped. If that didn't work, they were locked in a wooden box out behind the shed.

Book closed and locked the door. When her foot-steps died away, Sadie sat up. Her stomach cramped with hunger, but she didn't want to take food from the starving girls. But they both saved her a little, and she thankfully wolfed it down. Bread and milk was her very favorite thing.

"Don't they let you out to use the toilet?" Sadie asked.

"No. There's a slop bucket. Someone empties it each morning."

Sadie wrinkled her nose just thinking what a terrible smell there would be once the lid was removed. "Does that woman come back for the dirty bowls and spoons?"

Victoria shook her head. "Someone will get them in the morning."

Just then Sadie heard footsteps again.

"Who can that be?" Clarissa whispered.

"Maybe Mr. Wippet." Victoria shivered.

"Do what he says," Sadie whispered as she laid back down and tried to relax enough to breathe like Opal. Inside her head she said, "Relax, relax, relax." Silently she prayed that she wouldn't give herself

42

away. She knew God was with her, even in this awful place.

The door opened, and Horace Wippet walked in carrying a whip with three lashes—each twelve inches long.

The girls cried out and huddled closer together.

Sadie struggled to keep her eyes closed. Why were the girls so afraid?

"Good evening, Victoria, Clarissa." Horace looked grim. "Are you ready to begin working tomorrow?"

"Yes," they said together in weak voices even though they both longed to shout, "No!"

"Good! I was afraid I'd have to use this." He slapped the whip against the side of the door. The girls squealed and jumped. Sadie almost did too.

Horace walked to the bed and looked down at Sadie and Opal. "These girls won't cause any trouble for me. They're so trusting! It was easy to get them out here, and it'll be just as easy to get them to stay."

Sadie burned with rage, but she didn't move even an eyelash. She would not let Horace Wippet know she was awake!

Finally Horace walked to the door. "Tomorrow you girls will be working in the glove factory. You will not be allowed to go outdoors or talk to anyone. If someone visits the factory—perhaps Sadie's and Opal's father—you won't say a word to him. He must not learn the girls are here or I'll have to kill him."

Sadie felt hot, then icy cold. How she wanted to leap on Horace and knock him to the floor, take his whip, and use it on him!

"Sadie and Opal will stay locked in this room all day tomorrow, of course." Horace flicked the whip, and the lashes danced in the air. "Unless of course this scares them into instant obedience."

Just then a bug crawled across Sadie's hand. She felt a scream rising in her, but she bit it back. She wanted to brush it off, but she didn't dare. What kind of bug was it? A flea? A bedbug? A cockroach? Chills ran up and down her spine. Maybe it was only a fly or an ant.

"See you girls in the morning just after daylight. Our sleeping beauties will be awake by then." Horace chuckled and walked out, locking the door behind him.

Sadie gasped and flicked the bug off her hand. It landed on the floor, and Victoria squashed it flat with her foot.

Wrinkling her nose and curling her lip, Clarissa said, "I hate bedbugs!"

Bedbugs! Sadie shivered.

"The mattress is covered with them," Victoria said with a shudder.

Sadie jumped up and brushed at herself just in case any were on her. She saw one on Opal's cheek, and she flicked it onto the floor and stepped on it.

Just then a key grated in the lock. Sadie flew back to the bed. Could she really lie back down with the bedbugs? She had to! She dropped back in place just as the door opened.

Horace stood in the doorway with a frown. "What was all the noise?"

Victoria searched her mind for a good answer, then pointed to the floor. "Bugs! We were squashing them."

"They're awful," Clarissa whispered as she huddled close to Victoria.

"Yes, they are bad." Horace laughed. "I lived with my share back when I was an orphan in New York City." The laugh died on his face. "I came to take you girls to another room, but I think I'll leave

44

you here to enjoy the bedbugs one more night." He walked out and locked the door.

Sadie breathed a sigh of relief. Bedbugs were easier to deal with than Horace Wippet!

Suddenly Sadie had an idea. She pulled Opal's gloves from her petticoat pocket. She held the patched one out to Victoria. "Take this, and if Caleb York or anyone else comes looking for us, find a way to slip it in his pocket. Daddy will know it belongs to Opal, and he'll tear down this place until he finds us."

Victoria took the glove and tucked it into the pocket of her petticoat. "I'll try my best."

"I know you will." Sadie looked at the other glove, then handed it to Clarissa. "You do the same with this one if you can."

"I will." Clarissa took the glove with a shiver. "But I'm not brave."

"You'll be brave enough to do that. My daddy will get your pa, and they'll set us free!" Sadie lifted her chin and squared her shoulders. "We have a Heavenly Father too who watches over us. He'll help all of us!"

Sadie turned back to Opal. A small red bedbug crawled over Opal's foot. Sadie brushed it off and squashed it flat, and then she shivered. Oh, but she hated bedbugs!

5

The Black Cowboy

Opal groaned and slowly opened her eyes. Her mouth felt full of cotton, and her eyes were almost too heavy to open. Weak light poked through the cracks in the slats across the window. Sadie lay curled on her side next to her. Opal lifted her head, and the room spun, then righted itself. The room smelled like an outhouse! Where were they?

Opal gripped Sadie's shoulder and shook her. "Sadie! Wake up!"

Sadie sat bolt upright and remembered immediately where they were and what had happened to them. "Shhhh! Opal, whisper so nobody outside the room hears you."

Opal frowned. "Where are we?"

Just then Victoria and Clarissa woke up and scrambled to the side of the bed.

Opal gasped. She knew immediately who they

were from their pa's description of them. "Victoria and Clarissa Elston? Where are we?" It was hard to talk through her dry, dry mouth.

Sadie sat on the edge of the bed and tugged Opal to her side, then quickly told her all that had happened, with Victoria and Clarissa adding information now and then. They explained their plan for Opal's gloves, and she gladly agreed to it. Sadie ended by saying, "We have a plan for you to carry out too, Opal."

"I want to get out of here." Tears spilled down Opal's cheeks.

"We don't have much time to talk," Victoria said softly.

"Here's what you're going to do, Opal . . ." Sadie held Opal's hand tightly. "You're going to make Horace Wippet think he helped us out by having us stay the night after we 'fainted.' Ask him about himself and how he came to be here to run The Poor Farm. Get him to tell you his life's story so he won't be watching us as closely as usual. Butter him up like you do the other fine young men you want to impress."

Opal frowned. "Sadie, I don't do that!"

Sadie grinned. "You do too, and you know it. So, do it again to help us. We want the freedom to talk to others and get their help in an escape."

"We want to go home," Clarissa said with a break in her voice.

Victoria nodded. "We do."

Opal trembled as she thought about the daring plan. Could she carry it out? She'd have to! "I'll do it," she said just above a whisper.

A key grated in the lock, and the girls shivered. Victoria and Clarissa hurried to the wall and sat on the floor against it with their heads down. Sadie and

Opal sat on the edge of the bed and stared at the door. It opened, and Book walked in with a tray carrying bowls of bread and milk on it. A book filled her apron pocket. Without a word she passed the bowls around, then walked out and closed the door.

"I'll pray," Sadie said as she bowed her head. "Heavenly Father, thank You for this food. Give us strength for this day, and show us a way to escape. In Jesus' name, Amen."

"Amen," the others said.

The girls wolfed down the bread and milk and piled the bowls together at the side of the door with the spoons in the top bowl.

"Can God really help us?" Victoria asked fearfully.

"Yes, He can—and He will!" Sadie said with confidence. "Our daddy says God always know where we are and what's going on, and He always wants to help us and watch over us." But inside herself, Sadie wondered how God would help them this time.

As Sadie rebraided her hair, Opal combed her hair with her fingers and retied the ribbon around it. She felt dirty and wrinkled. She scratched the bites from the bedbugs, then shivered as she thought about the bugs crawling all over her during the night.

Just then a key grated in the lock again, and the door swung open. Victoria and Clarissa once again sat against the wall with their heads down as if they were totally defeated. Opal and Sadie perched on the edge of the bed. Horace Wippet stood in the doorway with his whip in his hand, a questioning look on his face. Behind him stood a powerfully built man with his arms crossed and a forbidding look on his face. He had hard-as-coal black eyes and shoulder-length black hair with a beaded band around his forehead that kept his hair out of his face.

"Horace, thank God!" Opal rushed to him and ignored the other man, who took a step forward. "I can't imagine what happened to us. I'm thankful we fainted here and not out in the prairie on the way to Starr! These girls told us the strangest story—that they're prisoners here! Why would they say that, Horace?"

He laughed nervously. "Orphans like to run free in the streets," he said gruffly. "I brought them here so they'd have a home."

"That's what I thought!" Opal sighed in relief. "I'm sorry we caused an inconvenience to you. Sadie and I must be going. But maybe we can see more of your place before we have to leave."

His brows raised, Horace looked at Opal, then laughed dryly. "Of course you can see more of the place. I came to see if you want to work or stay here in the room."

"Work, of course!" Opal turned to Sadie. "Do you, Sadie?"

Sadie nodded. She couldn't tell by Horace's face if he believed Opal's act. "I can help Rann again for a while . . . if I'm not too dizzy." She added the last sentence as a good touch. Was Horace falling for the act?

He snapped his whip toward Victoria and Clarissa. "Come here, girls!"

They jumped up and hurried over to him, looking very frightened.

"Are you girls ready to work?"

They nodded but didn't speak.

"You're going to work in the glove factory." Horace tapped Victoria. "You'll be a sorter." He tapped Clarissa. "And you'll be an inspector."

"What about me?" Sadie asked.

Horace scowled at her. "The first thing I want

you to remember is not to speak unless I speak to you."

Sadie hung her head to hide the flash of anger in her eyes. "Yes, sir."

Opal bit her tongue to keep back a sharp retort.

Horace flicked his whip in Sadie's direction. "You'll stay here."

"Here?" Sadie cried in surprise.

"You said you were dizzy."

"She'll be fine," Opal said quickly. "Besides, being out in the fresh air is good for her."

"If you say so." Horace took Opal's arm. She fought against the repulsion she felt for him and managed to smile. He turned to Sadie again. "You can go with these girls to the glove factory and help sort."

Relief washed over Sadie, but she didn't let it show.

Horace turned to the man in the doorway. "Tiffin, take the girls out and tell Stout what jobs to give them. Opal will stay with me."

Opal managed to smile.

With a grunt Tiffin motioned to the girls, then led them out into the bright sunlight. Sadie glanced around, but didn't see anyone who would help her. Once again the garden was full of quiet children hoeing and raking to prepare for planting. Rann was in the corral with Soot. He didn't look Sadie's way, and she didn't call out to him like she wanted to do. Had he given up all hope of her helping him get away?

Biting her lip, Sadie walked inside the small building that looked like a chicken house with windows and a wooden floor. Inside two men, three women, and several children were silently doing different jobs. The clatter of the knitting machines and the *clack clack* of the sewing machines were loud in the small room. The smells of dyes and wool and unwashed bodies wafted through the room and out the open windows.

Tiffin motioned to a short man with a deep scar across his jutting chin and a whip in his hand much like Horace carried. "Stout, these two are sorters, and this one's an inspector."

Stout grunted.

Tiffin walked back out, leaving the door open and the screen door closed.

Stout walked past the mender, machinist, yarn winder, dyer, and knitter and stopped at a bin of salt-and-pepper-speckled gloves. He explained to Sadie and Victoria how to sort them, then lay them in pairs on the table beside the bin. He showed Clarissa where to stand to inspect the finished gloves before they were boxed and shipped away.

"You work 'til noon, get off fifteen minutes for dinner, then work 'til near on dark when you get off for supper and bed." Stout rubbed a thin hand over his face, then touched his scar. "You do the same seven days a week." He flicked the whip in his hand. "You can't say a word. If you need to ask me a question, you ring this bell." He pointed to a small bell with a long handle sitting at the corner of the bin. "You get a smack with the whip for each word you say out of turn."

Sadie ducked her head and bit her bottom lip to hold back a cry of alarm. Just how long had the others been working here under these conditions? Rann had said none of them were paid. Why didn't the people of Starr do something about it? How could they not know what Horace Wippet was doing here at The Poor Farm?

Finally Stout walked away, and Sadie sorted the gloves as Stout had shown them. The minutes seemed like hours since she couldn't utter a word without being struck a blow with the whip Stout carried. Her legs ached from standing in one spot, and her stomach cramped with hunger. Rann had said nobody was fed much. She was used to eating three big meals a day. Soon she lost all track of time. She wanted to look at Victoria on the other side of the bin, but she didn't dare. It would be too easy to whisper to her.

Just then the screen door squawked, and Tiffin stepped in. He talked quietly to Stout, then hurried back out.

Sadie's heart stood still. Was it possible Caleb had come looking for them? Tears stung her eyes. He'd find them somehow. He had to!

Stout stopped at Sadie's side and gripped her arm. "Come with me."

Sadie forced back the questions clambering at the tip of her tongue.

Stout pushed Sadie into a corner behind a big wooden box. "You stay here until I say you can come out." He hurried away without another word.

Frowning, Sadie peered through the cracks between the slats of the box. As she watched, Horace walked in with the black cowboy beside him—the same black cowboy she'd seen in Starr! Sadie wanted to leap out and shout to the cowboy, but she didn't move a muscle. What if the man was working with Horace? She saw Horace and the cowboy talking, but she couldn't hear what they said over the noise of the machines.

As she watched, she saw Victoria step back and stumble. She caught herself by clutching the cowboy. She pushed Opal's glove into the front pocket of his denim pants, then jumped away from him, her face scarlet.

Sadie clamped her hand over her mouth. Had the cowboy asked about her and Opal?

Stout gripped Victoria and pushed her against the bin, then walked on with the cowboy as if nothing unusual had happened.

Sadie's legs almost buckled, and she locked her knees to stay standing. She had to see what else the cowboy did. If only she could peek around the box so he could see her! Would he even remember he'd seen her in Starr and that she'd waved at him?

After a long time the cowboy walked out. Stout yelled at Victoria, then strode behind the box and yanked Sadie out. "You can get back to work now."

Sadie hurried to the bin and picked up a glove. She peeked at Victoria. The girl barely tipped her head and smiled. Sadie's heart almost leaped through her faded calico dress. Victoria must be trying to let her know the black cowboy had indeed asked about them. If he knew to ask about them, then he knew Caleb was looking for them!

Maybe Caleb would find them before dinner and set them free!

At dinner Sadie slowly walked to the house in single file with the others. She frantically looked around for Opal, but couldn't see her anywhere. Where was she? Had Horace done something terrible to her?

In the house Sadie took her bowl of cornbread and beans, then followed the line outdoors. She sat in the shade of a tall cottonwood tree between two boys about her age. They didn't say a word, nor did they look at her. She glanced around for Victoria and Clarissa and finally spotted them sitting near each other. Rann sat between a couple of ragged men who looked ready to fall over. Rann caught Sadie's eye, then looked quickly down at his bowl. Sadie glanced around again. Where was Opal? She prayed for herself and Opal, just as she'd been doing all day. But she wasn't sure if her praying was doing any good.

Sadie's stomach knotted, and for a minute she couldn't eat. But her hunger overcame her anguish, and she wolfed down the cornbread and beans . She wanted more, but she knew not to ask—one bowl each was all they'd get.

Finally Book rang a bell that meant they were to pile their bowls on a table near the back door of the house, then get back to work.

Sadie waited while the others stood, then managed to get in line behind Victoria. Sadie leaned close to Victoria, but before she could whisper to her Stout snapped his whip. Sadie jumped. He'd snapped the whip at two women, but the warning had been enough to keep Sadie from whispering to Victoria. Sadie followed the line to the table, set her bowl and spoon down, then followed the line back to the glove factory.

Sadie's heart sank to her feet, and chills ran up and down her spine. Where was Opal?

6
Opal

Inside the huge barn Opal leaned against the pitchfork and groaned. Her back hurt, and her arms ached. She was used to hard work, but since early this morning she'd been cleaning out stalls, pushing the wheelbarrow loads to the garden where the workers mixed it in with the soil, wheeling the wheelbarrow back to the barn, and putting fresh straw in each stall. Pigeons cooed in the rafters, and dust danced in the sunlight filtering through the holes in the barn siding. She rubbed her dirty hand down her sweaty, damp skirt. This morning she'd been so sure Horace had fallen for her ploy, but when she'd walked away with him, he'd shown her to the kitchen.

At the doorway he'd smiled at her as if he knew something she didn't. "From what you've said, you're a good cook. I want feather-light pancakes, three

57

eggs over easy, bacon fried until it's crisp, and coffee that isn't so strong it eats the silverplate off a spoon."

Opal stared at him in shock, then managed to smile. "I'll be glad to make you breakfast. It's the least I can do since you put us up last night."

He shrugged. "When it's done, carry it to my private dining room and sit with me while I eat. Book will show you where it is." Horace tipped his head, smiled, and swaggered away with his whip at his shoulder.

Later she carried his food to him on a heavy silver tray. He motioned for her to sit across from him at his small table covered with a fine lace tablecloth. A crystal bowl with a lily floating in it stood in the center of the table. She longed to share the food, but he never offered, and she knew she didn't dare ask him to.

Smiling, Horace flipped the white linen napkin open and spread it over his leg, then picked up his fork. His brown hair was neatly parted in the middle and combed down on either side. His stiff white collar looked uncomfortable. The striped tie hung down the front of his white shirt and stretched inside his flowered vest. His gray jacket looked too warm for such a pleasant morning. "Tell me about your family, Opal."

She locked her icy hands in her lap and sat with her back very straight. Could she speak around the hard lump in her throat? "There are five of us. I'm the second born. My two brothers, two sisters, and I were all born in Douglas County. We had a fine farm with a fine frame house painted white. Momma kept a good garden, and she planted lots of flowers too." Opal could see the nicely laid out farm with the big fields and tidy fences—everything orderly just like Pa wanted. She cleared her throat and brushed away a tear. "Pa . . . died in a blizzard." She couldn't go on for a minute because of the memories flooding her. When she brought her feelings back into check she said, "Momma met Caleb York when he was there to sell a horse to Pa. When Caleb returned after Pa was . . . gone, Momma and Caleb fell in love and got married. He moved us to the edge of the sandhills near Jake's Crossing."

Horace nodded as he dabbed his mouth with his napkin. "Jake's Crossing . . . I've been there."

"You have? Maybe you know Caleb's ranch. It's the Circle Y."

"Can't say as I do." Horace bit off a piece of crisp bacon. "Ummm. Just the way I like it. Tell me about your brothers and sisters."

Opal trembled but continued, "Riley is seventeen. When he turns eighteen he'll move onto his own homestead not too far from the Circle Y. Riley didn't like being a farmer, but he loves ranch life. My other brother is Webster—Web. He's ten, thin as a rail, but strong. He works hard. He learned to rope the fence posts, so now he can even rope a calf."

"I want to know what your brothers and sisters look like. What kind of a house do you live in?"

"We live in a sod house—chunks of sod cut from the prairie. But Momma hates it because of the bugs and snakes and mice that crawl right through the walls into the house." Opal's mouth was dry, but she kept talking. Horace seemed to enjoy hearing all about the family. "Caleb—we call him Daddy—plays guitar and sings. Our pa never sang or talked much at all."

Horace finished the last bite of food and crossed his arms. "My pa and ma died when I was four, so I barely remember them. I lived on the streets of New York City. Know what that was like?"

Opal shook her head.

"I lived in fear! And I was hungry all the time." His eyes flashed with anger. "I hated being hungry! I hated being afraid all the time more. I was glad when the Children's Aid Society picked me up and put me on the orphan train. You heard of the orphan train?"

Opal nodded. She'd met two boys who had arrived on the train. The bold, brash boys had seemed out of place on the prairie.

With a faraway look on his face, Horace pushed back his plate and leaned his elbows on the table. "I finally got taken in by a farm family in Iowa." His eyes flashed with anger. "After two years they decided they didn't want me, so they kicked me out. Just like that! I was twelve." His jaw tightened. "I took to the streets in Omaha." He chuckled dryly. "That's in Douglas County. Who knows—we might've run into each other—me when I was in my teens and you when you were still in diapers."

Opal flushed.

"I finally met up with a man who taught me how to live by my wits and make money off others. I sort of fell into what I'm doing here. I came to Starr a few years back and came out here to see what The Poor Farm was all about." He laughed dryly. "It was a stinking hole! So I took it over and made it into the place it is today."

"And what is that?" Opal asked softly.

"My domain! I rule this place! All the people who live here and work here are my servants." He laughed. "I'm the king here! My servants make gloves in my glove factory, and my other workers sell them. They raise crops I sell along with milk and cream and butter and eggs."

Opal frowned.

"You frown? Why? I deserve all I can get after the life I lived! I deserve it all!"

"But what about the people who work for you? What do they deserve?"

"They have a roof over their heads and food in their bellies!"

"And freedom to come and go as they want?" She wanted to jerk back the words, but it was too late.

He leaped to his feet, sending his chair crashing back. Immediately Tiffin charged into the room, his gun in his hand. Horace waved a hand at Opal. "Take her to the barn, and put her to work cleaning the stalls!"

"But I must find Sadie and get back to Starr!"

"That's impossible! You're staying here to work, and so is your little sister!" Horace had brushed her aside as if she were a dreaded bedbug.

Opal's thoughts came back to the present, and she leaned against the pitchfork as she fought to keep from flinging herself to the floor and crying wildly. Horace had refused to allow her to eat dinner or to rest. She was so tired and thirsty, she could barely stand.

Just then Rann walked into the barn and stopped near Opal and out of sight of the door in case anyone looked in. "I warned your sister about this place," he said in a low, tight voice.

"I know." Opal hung her head. "I wouldn't listen to her when she said not to drink the water."

"Mr. Wippet fools a lot of people."

"I know!" Opal nodded. "We tried to get away, but we couldn't."

Rann peeked out a small window. He didn't see anyone in sight, so he turned quickly back to Opal. "A black cowboy on a big white horse came here this morning and asked about you."

Her eyes lit up. She didn't know a black cowboy, but maybe Caleb did. "Did you tell him anything?"

"I couldn't! Mr. Wippet was watching."

Opal groaned and struggled to hold back the tears. "Did he see Sadie?"

"No. They won't let any outsider see her."

Opal's heart sank. She wondered if Victoria or Clarissa had had a chance to put one of her gloves in the cowboy's pocket. She didn't say anything to Rann about it in case it would somehow get him in trouble. "Where's Sadie now?"

He pointed with his thumb. "In the glove factory."

"Did she get to eat dinner?"

"Yes."

"We thought we'd be able to get away." Opal's voice broke, and she couldn't go on.

"You'll never get away." Rann sounded close to tears. "I tried, and others have tried too. Mr. Wippet won't let anyone get out."

Suddenly Opal realized Rann was talking to her even though he wasn't allowed to. "Why are you talking to me?"

"Nobody's around to hear us. I made sure."

"Please tell me a way to get out of this awful place. There must be a way!"

He spread his hands wide in defeat. "We're all locked in at night. Anyone who might cause trouble is given something to knock him out. There is no way out."

Opal saw the beat-down look all over Rann, but then she remembered that God was always with her to bring her victory in any situation. She lifted her chin and forced back the fatigue. "God is with us! With His help we will get out!"

Hope flickered in Rann's eyes, then died. Slowly he turned and walked away, his head down, his shoulders bent as if he were carrying the whole Poor Farm on his back.

Opal ran over to him and caught his arm. "Don't go yet. Help me think of something to do. Why can't I just get on a horse and ride out of here?"

"Tiffin would stop you any way he could. The last man who tried was shot right out of the saddle. He's buried in the pasture."

Opal shivered. "We have to think of something!"

Just then Rann caught her close and hauled her into a stall. "Don't say another word. Tiffin's coming."

Opal nodded and grabbed the pitchfork, while Rann scrambled up on the manger and crawled up into the haymow.

Trembling, Opal scattered clean straw across the stall floor.

Tiffin stopped in the doorway and blocked out the sun with his bulk. "Come with me. Mr. Wippet sent for you."

Opal froze. What could he want? Had he seen her talking to Rann? She thought of his terrible whip and sank to the floor.

Tiffin hauled her to her feet and pushed her toward the door.

Opal sprawled in the dust outside the barn door. Her face burning with embarrassment, she pushed herself up. Horace walked toward her, flicking the whip as he came. She gasped, her heart roaring in her ears.

7
The Fight

Wearily Sadie walked out of the glove factory between two ragged women who smelled like they'd never had a bath. She probably smelled as bad. The sun had already gone down, taking the heat of the day with it. The windmill blades whirred in the wind. She felt something in the air—a tension worse than she'd felt before. Her nerves tight, she glanced around, then spotted Opal near the barn cringing away from Horace as he walked toward her flicking his whip. Sadie gasped. In a flash she sped across the yard toward Horace. Sand spit out behind her shoes. She'd been the fastest runner in school in Douglas County, beating even the eighth-grade boys. She was even faster now. Only the Pawnee warrior Good One had beat her in a footrace.

Before anyone could stop her, Sadie flung herself against Horace and knocked him to the ground face first. The whip flew from his hand. He cried out and twisted around, tossing her off him. She grabbed his hair with both hands and held on tight.

With a roar Tiffin lunged toward Sadie, but Rann leaped from the haymow and down onto Tiffin, knocking him to the ground. His gun flew against the side of the barn and landed in the dust beside the foundation.

Suddenly a roar went up from the boys, girls, men, and women as they swarmed across the yard toward Tiffin and Horace.

Horace screamed and shook himself. Sadie lost hold of Horace and landed near Opal. Wide-eyed and hand in hand, they both backed away until they bumped against the barn as they watched the mob jump on Horace and Tiffin.

Sadie leaned against Opal and whispered frantically, "Let's get out of here while we can."

Opal nodded, but she didn't know how far she could run, as tired and hungry and thirsty as she was.

They ran around the angry, fighting mass of bodies toward the trail that led across the prairie to Starr. Fresh energy rushed though them. Just as they passed the house Book blocked their way, a Colt .45 pointed right at Sadie. She gasped and stopped short, and Opal trembled beside her.

"Get back where you belong," Book commanded in a hard, rough voice. Her book was securely in her apron pocket.

Sadie's heart sank. She looked helplessly at Opal.

"Book, let us go, please!" Opal cried. "You want to be free too, don't you?"

"Get back there!" Book waved the Colt and pushed Opal.

"Let us go! Please!" Sadie said over her shoulder, feeling close to tears.

Suddenly a shot rang out, and Sadie jumped in fright.

Opal darted a look around, then saw Stout with a smoking six-gun. He dropped the gun in the leather holster at his side, uncoiled a bull whip, and cracked it at the crowd around Tiffin and Horace. The whip sounded almost as loud as the shot. Stout swung it again, and this time the tip of the whip cut into one of the big boys. He cried out in pain and stared in anguish at the line of blood on his arm.

Suddenly dead silence fell as everyone turned to stare at Stout.

Sadie stumbled, caught her balance, and stopped several feet from the crowd.

Opal darted a glance back at Book, then stopped beside Sadie. They looked at each other without a word, then over at the mute crowd. A chicken squawked, and the windmill creaked. The sounds seemed extra-loud in the great silence all around the yard. Finally Horace pushed himself up. His collar and tie were off, his nose was bloody, his clothes were covered with dirt and half torn off, and his tangled hair stood on end. He was a far cry from the impeccably neat man of moments before. Anger radiated out from him. Sadie reached for Opal's hand and held it tightly.

Horace slowly walked to the wagon beside the barn, climbed in the back, and faced everyone. He glared at Opal and Sadie a long time, then looked over the entire crowd. Finally he said in a voice livid with anger, "You will all pay for this!"

Sadie lifted her head and squared her shoulders. She looked right at Horace and shouted, "We will all go free!"

Stout cracked the bullwhip, but Sadie jumped back, and the lash only caught her skirt and cut a line in it as easily as a pair of scissors would have.

Horace lifted his hand, and Stout coiled the whip but held it ready.

Opal slipped her arm around Sadie and stood bravely beside her.

Trembling, Horace shook his finger at the girls. "You two will pay the most! You will be locked in the box until I say you can come out!"

Sadie's eyes flashed. "Caleb York will come for us!"

"Shut up!" Horace cried.

"He will find us!"

Stout swung the whip and caught Sadie's arm, leaving a line of red blood.

Sadie cried out in pain, but took a step toward Horace. "Caleb York will never stop looking for us! He is led by God, and he will find us!"

Horace trembled, and the crowd gasped.

Again Stout swung the whip. Opal shoved Sadie to the ground and covered her with her body, and the lash snapped over their heads. Sadie had never seen Opal so brave.

"Enough!" Horace shouted. "Book, lock the girls in the box *now*. And don't feed them!"

Book nudged Opal with her toe. "Get up, the both of you."

Opal stood and helped Sadie to her feet.

"I'm all right," Sadie said softly.

"No talking!" Book snapped.

"What will you do, shoot me?" Sadie faced Book squarely and said in a voice loud enough for everyone to hear, "Even if you kill me and bury my body, God will help Caleb York find me."

Book narrowed her eyes and waved the Colt. "Get goin'!"

Sadie turned and walked slowly beside Opal across the yard. Sadie caught Rann's eye and smiled. He smiled back.

"We'll be watching for Caleb York!" Rann shouted. "And when he comes, we'll tell him where you are! We all will tell him!"

"Yes!" cried the others.

Tiffin lifted Rann off his feet and shook him as if he were a rag doll. "You better shut up or you won't be alive to tell anybody anything!"

"You'll have to kill us all!" Victoria shouted, and several others agreed.

Horace's face darkened with rage. "No one will eat tonight! No one! And no one will eat breakfast. Then we'll see who talks and who doesn't!" He waved to Stout and to Tiffin. "Lock the trouble-making sisters away without water or food."

Her face white but her eyes flashing, Opal stopped near the wagon and looked up at Horace. With all the courage in her she said, "And how will anyone work if they're too weak to move? Who will make money for you then, Horace Wippet?"

He glared down at her, then swore and turned away.

Book jabbed Opal in the back with the gun barrel. "Get moving!"

A few minutes later Book opened the side of the wooden box that looked like it had been used for shipping equipment. The lumber was gray and splintered with age.

Sadie trembled, but bent down and crept into

the box. She sat down and wrapped her arms around her knees.

With tears stinging her eyes, Opal hesitated, then eased into the box and sat holding her knees just as Sadie was doing. The two girls completely filled the box.

Book slammed the door and slid the bolt in place, then walked away, the Colt .45 dangling at her side.

Sadie looked through the spaces between the boards. If it rained tonight, they'd get soaking wet. If the temperature dropped too much, they'd get cold.

"Home sweet home," Opal said with a tiny grin.

Sadie giggled. "Momma would be happy to live in the soddy if she first had to live in here."

They looked at each other and burst into tears. After a long time they dried their eyes with their skirts.

"Momma would say it doesn't do any good to cry," Sadie said with a catch in her voice.

"She'd be right." Opal took a deep, shuddering breath. "We won't give up hope, Sadie. Daddy will come."

"I know." Sadie knew it as well as she knew her name was Sadie Rose York. Caleb always called her Sadie Rose even though she'd told him many, many times she was only Sadie. Her telling him never stopped him. He'd only smile and keep right on calling her Sadie Rose.

Just then Sadie remembered the black cowboy and Opal's glove. "Victoria gave your glove to a man who came today and was asking about us."

"What man?"

"I don't know his name." Sadie told Opal about the cowboy and when she'd seen him. "Maybe he's

Daddy's friend, and maybe right this minute he's giving him the glove."

"I hope so." Opal's stomach growled. "I'm sure hungry, Sadie."

"Me too. If we were home right now, we'd be eating wild turkey Web shot, with lots of dressing and gravy and potatoes too."

"With milk to drink and freshly baked bread." Opal moaned and tucked in her stomach so hard it hurt.

The last light of day faded, and darkness surrounded the box. A cricket sang nearby, and off in the distance a coyote yipped, and another answered.

Sadie and Opal clasped hands. "God is with us even in this box," Opal whispered.

"I know," Sadie said in a tiny voice. She thought about the Sunday services at the sod schoolhouse and the singing that made the walls bulge out. "Let's sing, Opal . . . just like Paul and Silas in the Bible when they were locked in jail."

Opal swallowed hard and nodded.

Sadie tipped her head back and sang, "Count your blessings, name them one by one."

Opal joined in, her voice weak and wobbly at first, then strong.

The song floated out and away from the terrible box and through the open windows into the house where the others were locked. Soon the air was full of voices singing the song Sadie had started.

A shot rang out and echoed across the prairie. "Stop that singing!" Horace screamed at the top of his lungs.

Sadie giggled. The song faded, and all was silent. Then Sadie lifted her head again and sang a foot-stomping praise song Judge Loggia had made up.

Opal hesitated a second, then joined in.

The song rang out and sounded as if all the angels had joined in, even though only Sadie and Opal sang. When the song ended, the prisoners in the house clapped and cheered. Sadie and Opal leaned their heads together, closed their eyes, and soon drifted off to sleep.

8

Caleb York

In the darkness outside the livery, Caleb York leaned against his wagon and prayed for his girls, as he had constantly done since last night. Where were Opal and Sadie Rose? He pushed his hat to the back of his head and looked at the lights glowing from several of the buildings along the main street and from the houses scattered behind the street. Last night he'd knocked on every door to ask about the girls. He'd talked to *everyone*, but no one had noticed them except his old friend from Texas—Honey Wilson—and the clerk in the general store. Caleb smiled as he thought about yesterday afternoon when he'd walked out of the office at the lumberyard to find his tall black friend riding past. They hadn't seen each other for over six years.

"Wilson . . ." Caleb had called.

Wilson had reined in his big white horse and

turned, then leaped to the ground and grabbed Caleb in a bear hug. "York! I never thought I'd set eyes on you once you left Texas for good!"

"You're sure lookin' good, Wilson." Laughing happily, Caleb slapped Wilson's back. He went by Wilson because of the teasing he got when he told anyone his first name—Honey. His momma had given him that name when they were still both slaves. After the Civil War ended and Wilson was a free man, he moved to Texas to work on the same ranch Caleb worked on. Wilson never told anyone his first name except Caleb—after they became friends!

"You're a sight for sore eyes, York!" Wilson had never heard Caleb called anything but York, so Caleb explained how after he was married he decided he'd like a first name like everybody else. His family had chosen Caleb from the Bible, after Joshua and Caleb, the two spies who gave a good report of the Promised Land when Moses was leading his people to freedom. Wilson said he'd stick with calling him York since it would be too hard to change.

"Me and my girls will be in town only for the night. Can you come with me to get my girls and have some supper?"

"Sure can." Wilson tied his horse to the wagon and fell into step with Caleb. "Where your girls at?"

"Walkin' around lookin' at everything if I know my girls." Caleb told Wilson about falling in love with the most wonderful woman in the world, then marrying her. "I'm in town to get the lumber to build a frame house. Are you married yet, Wilson?"

"Would be if she'd have me."

They'd talked as they walked. Soon Caleb started getting nervous about not finding Opal and Sadie Rose. He started asking around. After he'd described the girls, Wilson had told him about seeing them in a wagon with a man heading out of town. Caleb had learned from the clerk at the general store that the man was Horace Wippet.

"I'm going right out there," Caleb said sharply.

The clerk smiled. "Horace Wippet will do all he can to help find your girls. Might be he was giving them a ride somewhere. He's generous to a fault."

Caleb had hurried out to the wooden sidewalk with Wilson beside him. "I'm going to The Poor Farm to talk to this Horace Wippet. I'll get a horse and go now. Will you keep looking around town?"

Wilson had nodded. "Sure will."

But Caleb hadn't learned a thing. He'd talked to Horace Wippet outside the house that seemed unusually quiet.

"I dropped the girls off at the edge of The Poor Farm property," Wippet had said. "They said they were going to visit a friend."

Caleb had left without arguing. He'd known Wippet had lied, but he didn't know why. He still didn't know why as he stood beside his wagon and waited for Wilson.

Just then Caleb heard the *clip clop* of a horse coming toward him. He straightened up and looked toward the sound. He saw the flash of white of Wilson's big, beautiful horse. "Anything, Wilson?" Caleb called.

Wilson waited until he reached the wagon and slid off his horse. He left the reins dangling and turned to his old friend York.

"I went to that Poor Farm like I said I would, but they never saw hide nor hair of them girls of yours. I seen two girls who looked like you said yours looked, but they weren't your gals."

Caleb gripped the butt of his Colt .45. "How'd you know?"

"Both them girls had dark eyes." Wilson chuckled. "'Course not as dark as mine, but near on.'"

Caleb frowned. "Sounds like Scott Elston's girls. Elston seemed like a good man. I can't figure out why his daughters ran away from him."

"One of them girls fell against me, even stuffed a glove in my pocket. I never could figure out why she'd do such a crazy thing."

"What kind of glove?"

"Just a glove." Wilson shrugged. "I was in the glove factory where they make 'em."

Caleb sighed in disappointment. "I'll check out Mr. Horace Wippet again tomorrow. Why would the girls get in his wagon and ride with him? Why'd he say they were going to visit someone? They don't know anyone in these parts."

"He said he's always pickin' up folks and giving 'em rides. He didn't recall who your girls were going to see. He seemed honest enough."

"The town's people think good of him. But I reckon I'll pay a call on him anyway. We might run across them Elston girls and talk 'em into going back home where they belong."

"We can't do anything more tonight." Wilson pulled off his big white Stetson and rolled the brim nervously. "York, I need your help."

"You got it."

"With a stubborn woman."

Caleb laughed. "I don't know if I can help there."

"You stayin' at the Cray Hotel tonight?"

"Yes."

"Indigo, the woman I plan on marrying up with, works for Cray, the hotel owner. He treats her like a slave."

76

Caleb frowned. "Why does she stay with him?"

Wilson rammed his hat back onto his head. "She's scared to leave him. And she's scared to marry up with me since I'm just a cowboy."

"Then stop being just a cowboy! There's land near my place you can homestead. Maybe that would suit her more."

Wilson laughed. "Could be! Let's talk to her and see."

A few minutes later Caleb sat across from Wilson at a small square table with a red-and-white checkered tablecloth. The room was lit by several lamps and smelled of steak and freshly baked bread. Caleb glanced around the almost empty room in hopes of seeing Opal and Sadie Rose. They weren't there, and his heart sank. He couldn't leave Starr until the girls were with him. He'd find them no matter how long it took him! He silently asked God to please help him find the girls. He knew God had helped him get through tough situations before, and He would help him now!

Wilson nudged Caleb and nodded his head toward a slender black woman wearing a white muslin dress with a red brooch at her throat. "That's Indigo Ashley."

Without smiling, Indigo stopped at the table. Red combs held her curls back off her face. "Wilson, I told you to leave me be," she whispered.

"Did I come to see you, gal? I came to get food for me and my friend York. We worked the same ranch in Texas a while back."

Indigo turned her dark eyes on Caleb. "You a cowboy too?"

"I was, but I have my own place west of here— the Circle Y Ranch."

"He got himself a wife and five young 'uns."

Wilson motioned to the chair beside him. "Sit a spell and talk, Indigo."

"I can't!"

"You been working all day. You can take time with friends."

Indigo darted a look over her shoulder and finally sat down. She turned to Caleb again. "You the man who lost his girls?"

Caleb nodded. "Wilson here said he saw them riding out of town with Horace Wippet."

Indigo gasped. "Then you won't never see them again."

Caleb's stomach knotted. "What do you mean by that?"

Indigo shrugged. "I shouldn't have said that. Forget I did." She started to stand, but Caleb caught her wrist and forced her back down. He released her, and she rubbed her wrist and frowned.

"I'm sorry if I hurt you." Caleb forced himself to stay calm. "I'm just scared for my girls. But why is it that everybody in town has a good word for Wippet except you?"

She shrugged.

Wilson took Indigo's hand in his and smiled into her eyes. "Tell us, girl. It's mighty important."

"Life and death," Caleb whispered.

Indigo took a deep breath and fingered the brooch at her throat. Her skin gleamed in the lamplight, and her teeth flashed white as she opened her mouth. "Wippet does some business with my boss Cray, and sometimes they talk and drink together. Wippet don't want it known that he drinks, but he sometimes goes away from here barely able to walk."

"Okay, he drinks. Lots of men drink." Caleb watched Indigo closely. He knew she had more to say but was afraid to talk. "What else?"

"He says he's king at The Poor Farm—he rules the place with a whip, he says."

Caleb's jaw tightened, and it was hard not to leap up and head for The Poor Farm even at such a late hour.

"Tell us all you know, Indigo," Wilson said softly.

She looked for Cray, but he wasn't in sight. "He says he keeps prisoners there. And he never pays them for the work they do."

Caleb had all he could do to keep seated. "Why didn't you or Cray tell anyone else?"

Indigo swallowed hard. "You're gonna cause a heap of trouble for me."

"Think of my girls," Caleb said in a tight voice.

"Cray won't tell because he can get goods from Wippet at bare cost." Indigo shrugged. "Nobody would believe me if I said anything. Wippet's almost a god to folks around here."

Caleb's head spun. He wanted to rush to The Poor Farm, but he knew it wouldn't do any good.

Just then Cray walked into the room. He was a heavy-set man with a round, red face and a bald head. He motioned impatiently to Indigo, and she jumped up.

"Bring us steak and potatoes with apple pie and coffee," Caleb said.

Indigo nodded.

Wilson caught her hand and grinned. "I'll stop in tomorrow morning to talk you into marrying me. York here says we can homestead near him. I can be ready to leave when he does. I want you ready too."

Indigo scowled at Wilson and walked away.

Caleb laughed. "I think she'd like a little more romance, Wilson. Give her some sweet talk, then get on your knee and declare your love for her, then ask her to marry you and live with you forever."

Wilson frowned. "I ain't much for sweet talk."

"You'd better learn it or you won't get that fine woman to marry you." Caleb found it hard to talk about anything but what Indigo had told them, but Cray was standing nearby, so they didn't dare say a word about Wippet.

Later Caleb and Wilson walked back to the livery. Caleb rested his hand on Wilson's shoulder. "Friend, I'm hitchin' up my team and ridin' for The Poor Farm right now. I'd be pleased if you came with me."

Wilson chuckled. "Like old times—fighting side by side. Sure, I'll go with you. But I got to be back here tomorrow to convince Indigo to marry me."

Caleb awakened the man at the livery so he could tell him he was taking Dick and Jane. He hitched them to the wagon and drove away with Wilson riding alongside on his white horse.

Outside The Poor Farm Caleb stopped behind a hill so they couldn't be seen. Wilson tied his horse to the back of the wagon and untied his bedroll from behind the saddle. He tossed the bedroll under the wagon, then unhooked his gunbelt. He pulled the glove from his pocket and laid it up on the wagon seat.

"I'll check the place out before beddin' down," Caleb whispered. They both knew their voices would carry on a quiet night.

Wilson fell into step beside Caleb. "I reckon I'll go with you."

A few minutes later they stood to the side of the dark, silent farm. A horse nickered. Caleb's heart raced. Were his girls somewhere on the farm?

Finally they walked back to the wagon and

crawled under it to sleep. Long after Wilson fell asleep, Caleb lay awake, silently praying for Opal and Sadie Rose.

"No matter where you girls are, I'll find you," he vowed in a low voice.

9
Locked In Again

Sadie moved and bumped her head against the box, then awoke with a start. She ached all over, and she was weak with hunger. She turned her head to find Opal awake and close to tears. Daylight streaked the eastern sky, but the sun wasn't up yet. Birds twittered in the nearby cottonwood trees.

In frustration Sadie kicked at the boards. She already knew the boards were too strong to break. During the night they'd awakened and tried. Then Opal had tried to reach the lock, but after trying for several minutes she'd finally given up.

Sadie drew her knees tight to her chest. "I can't stay in here any longer!"

"Me either. I should've stayed home like I always do! Why did I pick this time to come?" Opal's face was streaked where tears had made clean trails down her dirty cheeks. "I am so hungry!"

A hunger pang stabbed Sadie. "Maybe they'll feed us today."

"Maybe." Opal brushed hair from her eyes. "Horace seemed too angry to ever let us eat again."

Just then they saw Tiffin and Stout walk out of the house toward them. They shivered. Were they coming to kill them? Or maybe they were going to let them out so they could eat. Sadie's mouth watered at the thought.

Tiffin slipped back the bolt and hauled Opal from the box. Her legs gave way, and she crumpled to the ground. Flushing, Opal tried to stand, but couldn't after being in the same position all night. She felt like a newborn foal trying out its legs for the first time.

Stout pulled Sadie out, and she tried to stand, but her legs wouldn't support even her slight weight. She started to fall, but Stout caught her and flung her over his shoulder, just as Tiffin did with Opal.

"Where are you taking us?" Sadie asked in alarm as blood rushed to her head.

"Mr. Wippet wants you locked in the barn so you'll know when Caleb York comes but won't be able to do anything about it." Tiffin chuckled. "Mr. Wippet always gets his way."

Sadie shivered, and Opal whimpered. Opal closed her eyes, but Sadie kept hers open to see if she could see anyone—maybe Caleb coming to rescue them. The world looked strange upside-down. There was no sign of Caleb. She tried to remind herself he'd be coming, but her heart sank in despair. Then she remembered Opal's glove, and hope sprang high again.

Inside the dark barn Tiffin opened the tack

room door and dropped Opal inside near a bench. She cried out in pain, then sneezed from the dust that rose around her. Before she could move, he bound her wrists behind her back, tied her ankles securely, then forced a red bandanna between her lips and tied it in back of her head. She tried to shout, but she couldn't utter more than a garbled sound.

Sadie closed her eyes as Stout bound her wrists and ankles.

"Caleb York will come!" Sadie cried more to remind herself than the men.

"We're counting on him coming." Chuckling wickedly, Stout tied Sadie's bandanna, pushed her to the floor, and pointed to a crack in the wall where the wood had weathered and pulled apart. "You can watch your Caleb York right through there but won't be able to do a thing about it."

As the men walked out, Sadie thrashed about, but finally stopped in defeat. The ropes and bandanna were too tight. She couldn't speak, and she couldn't get free. She couldn't kick the barn siding to try to break out or draw attention because the rope that bound her wrists was tied to the rope around her ankles. She whimpered. The room smelled of leather and saddle oil as well as dust.

At a sound from behind her, Sadie turned to see Victoria and Clarissa lying on the floor, bound and gagged in the same way. Their eyes were big and round and full of questions. Sadie bumped Opal with her head and nodded toward the girls. Opal looked, and her eyes widened in surprise. She tried to speak. Saliva filled her mouth and soaked into the bandanna, leaving her tongue dry and uncomfortable.

Sadie motioned with her head for the girls to come to them so they could watch through the opening. Finally they understood and inched across the dirt floor. The girls peered through the opening and waited for Caleb York.

Outside the farm Caleb and Wilson crept around the base of the hill until The Poor Farm was in full sight. Smoke rose from the chimney at the east end of the house. Two men, one tall and the other short, walked from the barn toward the house and disappeared inside. The windmill stood in silence even though a light wind was blowing. There was no other activity for a while, but then a line of silent people walked from the house in single file. Some went to the garden, a few to the barns, and others to the glove factory.

Caleb frowned. "I don't see Sadie Rose or Opal."

"I don't see them Elston girls either," Wilson whispered.

Caleb jumped up. "Let's have a talk with Horace Wippet!"

"We can't let him know we're suspicious of him," Wilson said sharply.

"You're right." Caleb took a deep breath to calm himself. Silently he prayed for help in dealing with Wippet. Caleb clamped a hand on Wilson's shoulder. "Ready, friend?"

"Sure am!" Wilson settled his white hat in place and touched the butt of his gun.

Caleb walked boldly to the door of the house where he'd watched the stream of people come out. He knocked, then glanced around. He saw a boy leading a horse to the corral, but the boy didn't take any notice of him. Caleb frowned. Why didn't the boy call out to him or wave or smile?

The door opened, and Book stood there with a

scowl on her face. Smells of frying food drifted out around her. "What d' you want?"

"To speak to Horace Wippet." Caleb wanted to push the woman aside, but he held himself back.

"He'll be right out." She slammed the door in Caleb's face.

Shaking his head at her rudeness, Caleb walked away from the house with Wilson beside him. They scanned the area, looking for the girls again.

Inside the barn Sadie's heart jumped, and she tried to shout so Caleb could hear her. Finally she gave up trying and watched him standing with the tall black cowboy. He must've given Caleb Opal's glove! Caleb would know for sure they were there! Soon they'd be free, and Horace Wippet would be carried off to the nearest town with a jail!

Opal's eyes filled with tears, and she blinked them quickly away so she wouldn't miss anything. Inside her head she cried, *Daddy, look here at the barn! We're locked in and tied up! Look here, Daddy!*

Frowning slightly, Caleb looked toward the barn. Had he heard someone cry for help? He turned as the door of the house opened and closed.

Horace Wippet walked out, smiling and looking as immaculate as ever. Anger, and even a touch of fear, rushed through him at the sight of the two rugged men, but he didn't let it show. "What brings you men out here so early in the morning?"

Caleb tried to smile but couldn't. "My girls are still missing. Have you seen them at all since the other evening?"

Horace shook his head. "I wish I could say I have. I know how it must feel to have loved ones just walk away from you."

Caleb knotted his fists. How he wanted to ram a fist in Wippet's face and make him tell the truth, but Caleb held back. He had no way of being sure that Wippet was lying. Maybe Indigo had misunderstood what what she'd heard Cray and Wippet say.

Inside the barn Sadie and Opal tried to shout, but couldn't get out a sound loud enough for Caleb to hear.

Wilson pushed his hat to the back of his head. "I want to ask those two dark-haired, dark-eyed girls I saw here yesterday a couple of questions."

"You must mean Victoria and Clarissa."

Caleb's heart stopped.

Wilson nodded. "Sure do."

"They heard their pa was looking for them, and they left here on the run so he wouldn't find them." Sadly Wippet shook his head. "I hate seeing families torn apart."

Inside the barn Victoria and Clarissa burst into tears. Anger toward Horace Wippet filled Sadie, and her heart hammered in her chest. She wanted to comfort the girls but couldn't. *Help me, God . . . Help us all.*

Wippet waved his hand to take in the farm. "I'll be glad to show you men around the place. We have hard-working people who are glad for a roof over their heads and good food to eat."

Caleb wanted to tell Wippet he'd heard differently from Indigo, but he held his tongue. It wouldn't do to cause trouble for her. Caleb motioned to the boy in the corral. "I'd like to ask him a few questions."

Wippet tensed. "You're welcome to, but he can't

talk. Had his tongue cut out by Indians when he was a boy."

Caleb shook his head. "No need to, then. We'll be going so we can look around Starr for the girls. Could be they're waiting at the hotel for me."

"Could be," Wippet said, smiling.

Inside the barn Sadie's heart sank. Opal moaned and closed her eyes. They couldn't bear to see Caleb walk away and leave them behind.

Sadie tried to cry out, "Don't go, Daddy!" But the words came out as mumbled sounds that nobody could understand. Besides, they weren't loud enough to reach Caleb.

Their hearts heavy, the girls watched Caleb and the big cowboy walk away from Horace Wippet and away from The Poor Farm.

Sadie bowed her head and whimpered.

10
Defeat

His stomach in a cold knot, Caleb started to climb into his wagon to drive back to Starr. He felt like forcing Wippet to let him search the entire Poor Farm. But without proof he had no right to do that.

Warm wind blew across the new grass and dried the dew on it. Overhead a hawk shrieked in the blue sky. Caleb turned to speak to Wilson just as a gust of wind blew Opal's glove off the seat and into the back of the wagon. Caleb didn't notice.

"Let's hook up with Scott Elston," Caleb said. "The three of us can cover a lot of ground."

Wilson nodded, then grinned. "I'm seeing Indigo this morning. Maybe she'll want to help us look."

Caleb grinned. "Make sure you don't talk marriage to her without using a little sweet talk."

Wilson tugged his hat low on his forehead to

hide his embarrassment. "I've been givin' it some thought."

Caleb climbed in the wagon and flicked the reins. "Get up, Dick and Jane! We've got to find Opal and Sadie Rose."

At The Poor Farm Horace Wippet walked into the tack room and laughed down at the girls. "Caleb York came all right." Horace laughed harder. "But he left."

With a muffled cry, Sadie squirmed around angrily, hoping to work herself free. Finally she gave up and glared at Horace.

He sat on the bench and smirked down at the girls. "I suppose you're wondering why none of my people spoke up while Caleb York and the black cowboy were here."

The girls had been wondering that very thing, especially after last night.

Looking pleased with himself, Horace flicked his whip. "I told them that if they kept quiet I'd feed them fresh venison—all they could eat, plus four different vegetables, desserts galore, and milk by the gallons."

Sadie's mouth watered, Opal cried out in anguish, and the Elston girls moaned.

"I bet you girls are hungry, aren't you? As soon as you're ready to cooperate with me, you can eat all you want too." With another laugh, he walked out, locking the door behind him.

Feeling defeated, Sadie lay on the floor on her side for a long time. What could they do now? Maybe they should give up. No! She would never give up! God was on their side!

Sadie lifted her head. She could see Opal lying on her side with her back to Sadie. Suddenly an idea popped into Sadie's head. She could lay back to back with Opal and try to untie her hands.

Shivering, Sadie inched toward Opal. This had to work! *Please, God!* Sadie finally found Opal's hands. Opal jerked, then lay still when she realized what Sadie was doing. Sadie's fingers ached from working on the knot, but she kept working until she couldn't do it a minute longer. Defeated, she finally gave up.

Opal felt Sadie's defeat and reached out for Sadie's ropes. In determination Opal picked at the knots until her fingers burned, but she kept going. She felt a wetness on her fingers and knew they were bleeding, but she kept working anyway. She'd never worked at anything so hard in her life. She'd often untied stubborn knots in thread to keep from wasting it. Momma would never let them waste anything.

Suddenly Opal felt the knot loosen. She tried to cry out, but her mouth was so dry she couldn't. She patiently picked at the knots until finally Sadie's hands were free.

Sadie's heart leaped as she felt the rope fall down to her feet. She untied her gag and licked her lips and teeth until they were moist enough that she could close her mouth. She wanted to shout, but she didn't dare take a chance on anyone hearing her. "I'm going to untie your gags," she whispered. "But don't talk above a whisper. We don't want anyone checking on us."

She took the gags off the girls and tossed the bandannas on the bench. "I'll try to untie your hands now, but I'm not as good with knots as Opal."

"Get me loose first, then I'll get the girls free," Opal whispered. Oh, but it felt good to be able to close her mouth again!

Soon the girls were free and could rub their sore wrists and ankles.

Clarissa peeked through the crack in the wall. Nobody was in sight. Finally she turned to the others. "What'll we do now?"

"We better try to get out of the barn before somebody comes to get us," Sadie said as she looked around the room for a possible way of escape.

In Starr, Wilson walked into the diner. Smells of breakfast filled the room and drifted out onto the street. Frowning, Wilson looked around for Indigo. Maybe it was too early for her. He stopped the girl hurrying toward him with a tray of dirty dishes. "Miss, could you tell Indigo I want to see her?"

The girl shook her head impatiently. "She don't come in 'til mid-morning."

Wilson slowly walked out. He'd already stopped at the tiny house where Indigo lived. He'd knocked, but Indigo hadn't answered, so he'd figured she was already at work. Maybe he'd find her on the street or in one of the stores. He couldn't take much time to look for her. He'd take a quick look up and down the street, then ride to meet Caleb at the agreed place.

Several minutes later Wilson stopped beside the livery, scratched his head, then clamped his hat back on. Indigo had disappeared just like Caleb's daughters and the Elston girls. Was it possible Horace Wippet had her? Wilson shook his head. Why would Wippet take her? Unless he'd learned about her talk with them last night!

Just then Cray rode up to the livery on a buckskin mare. With his bulk and short legs he looked out of place on the back of a horse. He tipped his hat to Wilson, then left the horse for the boy at the livery to tend.

"Morning," Wilson said. He'd have to be careful what he said. "Could you give Indigo the day off so me and her could go on a picnic?"

Cray's round face reddened even more. "Indigo walked out on me, so I can't give her the day off. She got on the stage this morning and rode off."

Wilson's heart plunged to his boots. "Then I'll have to ride after her, won't I?"

Cray shrugged and walked away.

Wilson rode to the lumberyard, which was also the stage stop, left his horse at the hitchrail, and hurried inside to ask about Indigo.

"I wasn't here when the stage left," Michael Treet said. He turned to the middle-aged man across the office. "Gil, you see Indigo leave on the stage this morning?"

Gil nodded. "Dressed real pretty too."

Wilson sighed and turned to leave.

"Did Caleb York find his girls yet?" Mike asked in concern.

"Not yet."

"Mighty peculiar." Mike ran his fingers through his blond hair. "I been asking around for 'em too, but didn't get nowhere. I might head out to The Poor Farm today and ask."

"We already been there. No sign of them girls."

"Maybe we could get all them folks at The Poor Farm to help us look. Could be the girls got lost out on the prairie."

Wilson nodded. "I'll tell York your idea. We sure know they didn't go visitin' like Wippet said. They don't know a soul around these parts."

Mike frowned. "Why would Mr. Wippet lie?"

Wilson shrugged and walked away. He wanted to ride after Indigo and the stage, not meet York.

Why would Indigo just up and leave that way? It didn't make sense.

His heart heavy, Wilson mounted his horse and rode out to meet Caleb York.

At The Poor Farm Sadie sank down onto the bench. "It's no use. We can't get out of here."

Opal turned from peering through the crack. "At least we aren't bound and gagged. The corners of my mouth still hurt from the bandanna!" She rubbed the corners of her mouth, then her wrists.

Her eyes sparkling with tears, Victoria sat beside Sadie. "Will Caleb York come back?"

"Yes!" Sadie had to believe he would or she'd give up totally.

"Our pa doesn't come back anymore," Clarissa said with a catch in her voice. She'd been trying to dig a way out of the barn. "Maybe yours will stop coming too after a while."

"He won't," Sadie whispered, but she didn't sound very sure at all.

11
Indigo

Her nerves tight, Indigo Ashley inched as close to the big barn at The Poor Farm as she could get. Early that morning she'd taken the stage out of Starr, but had asked to be left off just beyond The Poor Farm. With her pack in her hand, she'd walked to the seclusion of a few cottonwood trees along a creek and changed into a pair of man's pants and a dark shirt. She'd lifted the broken-down .22 rifle from her pack, clicked it back together, and loaded it. She wasn't a good shot, but the rifle would give her some protection. Last night, after talking to Wilson and York, she'd devised a plan of her own to see if the girls were being held prisoner at The Poor Farm. It was high time she did something about Horace Wippet!

She heard the children hoeing and raking the garden plot that was longer and wider than the main street of Starr. They weren't talking or laughing. What would they do if they saw her? She eased back down to the ground. She couldn't take a chance. One shout and Wippet would be after her and take her prisoner. She shivered at the terrible thought.

Just then she heard voices. Cautiously she lifted her head. A tall, powerfully built man wearing an Indian headband and a woman with scraggly light brown hair and a book in her apron pocket stood several feet away in deep conversation.

"I won't stay here no longer, Tiffin! I told you that last fall, but you talked me out of leavin'. You can't talk me out of it again."

Tiffin gently brushed back her hair and kissed her. "Book, you know what Wippet will do if you try to leave."

"Not if you help me sneak away in the night. Wippet will never know you helped me." Book brushed Tiffin's hands aside. "I love you, Tif, but I can't tolerate seeing the agony of all them kids."

Indigo's breath caught in her throat. Things were worse than she'd thought!

"Give me a few more days, Book. Wippet's selling a shipment of gloves and will be busy with that. We can slip away together and be long gone before he misses us."

Book shook her head. "After hearing them songs last night, I remembered all them years my pa taught me from the Bible." She brushed tears off her lashes. "I prayed for the first time in a long time last night, and I promised God I wouldn't hurt nobody another day."

A blade of grass tickled Indigo's nose, and she almost sneezed. She pinched her nostrils together and moved enough to get away from the tickling grass.

Tiffin glanced around, then turned back to Book. "That singing was just fine, but it sure did anger Wippet. He was ready to kill them girls, but I talked him out of it. I don't hold to no killing."

Book pressed her work-roughened hand to her throat. "I'm supposed to be in that kitchen cooking that good food he promised the lot of 'em. But he said it would be cornbread and beans again today. He said it's all they deserve." Book's eyes flashed. "If Caleb York stops in again today, I'll tell him myself his girls are locked right there in that barn. Wippet can beat me if he dares, but I'm still telling!"

Indigo's heart raced. The girls were indeed there!

"Shhh!" Tiffin pulled her close and held her tight. "Don't you let nobody hear you—especially not Stout. He's loyal to Wippet."

They talked a while longer, then crept away, going their separate ways. Her heart racing at what she'd learned, Indigo inched over to a row of bushes where she'd have a better view of the area. Just then she noticed a boy riding a horse inside the corral. Was he high enough that he could look down and see her? She crawled closer to the bushes, then stopped. What if she ran into a rattlesnake? They could be out of hibernation already. Chills ran down her spine, and she wanted to leap up and run, but she stayed down. Dried leaves crackled under her, and she froze in place. Would the boy hear the crackle over the horse's hooves and the creak of the saddle? After a long time she crept from the protection of the bushes to the back of the barn. Could she get inside and find the girls?

Taking a steadying breath, Indigo pressed against the barn and inched along the back, careful her rifle didn't bump against it. She reached the

door, listened carefully, then slipped inside. She
darted to the first stall and listened again. Pigeons
cooed in the rafters, and a cat meowed in the stall
across the aisle. Indigo walked slowly to the next
stall. Sweat stung her skin.

A few minutes later she spotted the locked tack
room door. Her heart leaped. The girls were probably inside.

Gripping the rifle in her right hand, she ran
lightly past a buggy with barrels stacked near it and
over to the door. She inched the bolt back and eased
open the door. Four girls stood inside, staring at her
in fear.

Sadie stepped back from the black woman with
the rifle. "Who are you?" she said sharply.

"Shhhh!" Indigo held her finger to her lips, then
whispered, "I came for Caleb York's girls."

All four girls rushed forward.

Just then Indigo heard someone coming. She
urged the girls to hurry out, then closed and locked
the door. They ducked out of sight behind the pile of
barrels near the buggy just as Horace Wippet and
Tiffin walked in. They stopped outside the tack room
door.

Wippet slapped the whip against his hand.
"Josh better be wrong about seeing somebody
sneaking around out here."

"You can see the door's still locked," Tiffin said.

Just then Clarissa sneezed. The girls froze, and
Indigo's heart stopped. Clarissa pinched her nose to
keep from sneezing again. Sadie prayed they wouldn't
be found.

"Who's there?" Wippet cried angrily. "Check it
out, Tiffin!"

Indigo thrust the rifle into Sadie's hand and
stepped from behind the barrel. She walked right up

to Wippet. "It's only me, Mr. Wippet. I heard from Cray there was strange things going on out here, and I came to see for myself."

Wippet and Tiffin stared at her, too shocked to speak.

"But I checked out the place and couldn't see a thing wrong! I should've known, Mr. Wippet." Indigo headed for the outside door. "I guess my curiosity is satisfied. I can go back to Starr feeling good about this place."

Sadie listened intently as Horace asked, "What did Cray say to make you so curious?" Sadie wanted to peek around the barrels as Indigo answered, but she didn't dare take the chance of being seen. The other girls stayed very still in frozen silence.

Outside the barn Indigo walked toward the corral where Rann was working Soot. "Mr. Wippet, that's a fine animal. Is he for sale?"

"Yes." Horace leaned against the corral and watched Rann. "Are you in the market for a horse?"

"Yes. What are you asking?"

"Three hundred and fifty."

"That's more than I can pay." Indigo walked slowly away from the corral toward the trail that led back to Starr. "But that animal is worth every bit, I'm sure."

Horace nodded as he fell into step beside Indigo. Tiffin followed a few feet behind. Suddenly Horace caught Indigo's arm and stopped her. "How'd you get here?"

Indigo forced back a shudder. "I walked. I enjoy walking."

"I'll have Tiffin escort you to town." Horace motioned to Tiffin. "Take care of her."

Tiffin nodded. He knew Wippet meant for him to take her prisoner too.

Horace tipped his hat and hurried toward the glove factory.

With chills running up and down her spine, Indigo turned to Tiffin and said in a quiet voice, "I heard you and your friend Book talking. Get me out of here safely and I won't tell Wippet what I heard."

Tiffin tensed, glanced back at Wippet, then took Indigo's arm. "You'll have to get out of Starr, or he'll send Stout after you."

Indigo nodded. She hurried along beside Tiffin until they were out of sight around a hill. "If I were you, I'd get Book and leave that place as soon as possible."

He tipped his head in agreement.

"You won't want to be here when Caleb York returns. Go on back. I can get to town on my own." Indigo smiled, then ran down the trail toward town. She'd find York and Wilson as soon as possible and tell them what she knew.

Then she remembered her rifle. She'd left a loaded rifle with four girls! What if they hurt themselves—or someone else—with it?

12
Opal's Glove

Sadie peered through a crack in the barn and watched as Horace headed for the glove factory and Indigo, the black woman, walked with Tiffin on the road toward town. Sadie glanced down at the rifle. Was Indigo in danger from Tiffin?

Opal tugged on Sadie's sleeve. "We have to get out of here."

"I know." Sadie looked around the barn. Should they hide in the haymow until dark, then run to town for help so they could set the others free? She glanced at Victoria and Clarissa, then at Opal. They looked too weak to run anywhere. Sadie's legs trembled. She was weak too, but she would not let Wippet take her or the girls prisoner again!

Opal flipped her hair back, and her ribbon fell to the floor. She quickly picked it up and tied it back in place. "We don't dare go outdoors in daylight, so let's hide up in the haymow."

Sadie nodded and motioned toward the boards nailed to the side of the stall that led up to a square hole. Opal climbed up first, then Clarissa and Victoria. Before Sadie could follow them, Rann walked through the back door. He looked frightened and more ragged than before. Sadie froze in place. Rann hadn't seen her, but if she moved he would. And if he did see her, would he shout for Wippet? As she watched, Rann turned to look out the barn door. In a flash Sadie ducked behind the barrels. She held her breath, wondering what Rann was going to do.

In the haymow Opal locked her icy hands together. Where was Sadie? What had kept her from following them? They didn't dare call down to her in case someone heard.

Behind the barrels Sadie's back ached from the tension, and sweat dotted her face. She heard Rann coming toward her. Would he see her? Should she step out and confront him? Her legs refused to move.

Rann stopped at the tack room door, hesitated, and suddenly pulled the bolt back. He opened the door and whispered, "Sadie."

Her eyes wide in shock, she peeked around the barrels. "I'm over here."

Rann yelped, turned to face her, then looked back at the tack room door. He closed it and locked it again. "How'd you get out?"

She didn't want to tell him, so she asked, "Did you want me?"

He nodded. "I came to set you and the others free, and then I'm riding Soot out of here."

"Wippet will try to stop you."

Rann trembled. "I know, but this time I won't let him! I'd rather die than stay here!"

104

"Wait for Caleb York. He'll come help us all."

Rann shook his head. "I can't wait. Besides, he might not come, and even if he does, he might not help the rest of us."

"He will," Sadie whispered urgently.

Scowling, Rann rubbed his hands down his baggy pants. "I can't wait." He swallowed hard. "I'm . . . glad I got to meet you, Sadie."

Sadie smiled a shaky smile. "Me too. Come see us at the Circle Y near Jake's Crossing if you can."

"I will." He looked at her as if he were memorizing her, then ran out the back door.

Sadie dashed to the ladder and climbed awkwardly to the haymow with the rifle in her hand.

"What kept you?" Opal whispered fearfully.

"Rann." Sadie quickly told them about the meeting.

Her eyes wide in alarm, Victoria shook her head. "He'll run right to Mr. Wippet and tell him we're loose. I know he will!"

"He won't," Sadie whispered sharply.

"He will." Clarissa rocked back and forth. "You can't trust anyone in this place. He'll tell."

Sadie bit her lip. Would he? Right this minute was he running to Horace Wippet?

Opal moved close to Sadie and put her arm around her. "We have to trust someone, Sadie."

"I know." Sadie leaned her head against Opal's. But dare she trust Rann?

About the middle of the afternoon Caleb York stopped the wagon near the livery and waited for Wilson and Scott Elston. They'd stopped to talk to Mike Treet at the lumberyard to see if he'd seen the girls. Buggies and wagons rolled down the street, dust billowing out behind them. People walked on the sidewalks, busy with errands. Little groups of folks talked and laughed together. Caleb scowled at them. How could they laugh and talk when his girls were still missing?

He shook his head. He would not let himself feel that way! God was on his side! He'd find the girls and take them home safely!

Just then he looked over his shoulder at an approaching horse and rider. It wasn't anyone he knew, so he started to turn back. As he did, his eye caught something white in the back of the wagon. He jumped over the seat to see what it was, then gasped. "Opal's glove!" He picked it up and held it close. How had Opal's glove gotten in the back of the wagon? She would never leave it there to walk the streets. Someone had tossed it in the wagon, but who?

He glanced around, his eyes narrowed. How long had the glove been in the wagon?

Wilson and Scott Elston reined in beside Caleb's wagon. "What's wrong?" Wilson asked with concern.

Caleb held up the glove.

Wilson waved it away. "That's only the glove the girl at the glove factory pushed into my pocket."

Caleb couldn't speak for a minute. "It's Opal's glove," he said in a hoarse voice.

Wilson blew out his breath. "So the girls are there!"

Caleb rubbed an unsteady hand across his jaw, then climbed back onto the high seat. "At least they were."

"Suppose you explain to me what's going on," Scott said sharply.

Wilson quickly filled him in. "I reckon we'll head out to The Poor Farm to pay Mr. Horace Wippet another visit."

"I reckon we will." Caleb patted his Colt and checked his rifle. "We don't know who's on Wippet's payroll and who's against him. We'll have to be on the lookout on every hand."

Wilson touched his bullwhip and his six-gun. He was ready for anything.

Scott carried his rifle across his lap. "I'm not much of a shot, but I'll do what I can."

"Mike Treet would like to be in on this," Wilson said. "Seems like he took quite a shine to your girl Opal."

"We'll get him and head out there. We'll tear the place apart until we find our girls." His jaw set, Caleb lifted the reins and slapped them against Dick and Jane. God was answering his prayers!

At The Poor Farm Sadie peeked through the haymow window. She couldn't see Rann because the corral where he worked Soot was at the side of the barn. If only he'd wait until Caleb came, then he'd be safe!

But what if Caleb didn't come?

Sadie pushed the terrible thought aside. He would come!

What if Rann told on them?

Sadie pushed that terrible thought aside too.

On the floor several feet away from Sadie, Opal moaned and wrapped her arms around herself to ease the horrible pain. She had never been so hungry in all her life.

"What's wrong?" Victoria asked in concern.

"I'm hungry."

"Me too." Clarissa's face was white and her eyes dull. "I'm so thirsty, my tongue is thick."

Sadie heard the windmill turning in the breeze. Water was so close, yet so far away! Dare they try to get some water to drink? Better still, she could take a bucket from the barn and fill it with water for them all. Her heart raced at the daring plan. They couldn't get away as weak as they all were. She nodded. Yes, she'd get a bucket of water. Just thinking about a cold drink made her thirstier than she already was.

She looked at the rifle beside her. She couldn't carry both a bucket of water and the rifle. She shivered. Could she sneak to the well for water without the protection of the rifle? She had to!

"I'm going for water," she whispered.

The girls gasped and tried to talk her out of it, but she insisted she was going.

"I'll leave the rifle. Can any of you shoot straight?"

The Elston girls shook their heads. Opal said, "You know how I shoot."

Sadie did indeed. "Then don't shoot if you don't have to." Sadie crept to the square hole and peered down. If someone walked into the barn when she was climbing down the ladder, she'd be captured again, and so would the others. Dare she take that chance? She closed her eyes and moaned. She had to go, no matter what.

Silently she prayed for protection as she eased through the square hole and found the first board with her toes. She climbed down as quickly as she could, then dropped the rest of the way to the dirt floor. She waited, her heart in her mouth. No one walked in, and no one shouted out about the fugitive in the barn.

She picked up a bucket from beside the barrels and ran to the back door of the barn. It would've been quicker to go out the front door, but too dangerous. She wiped sweat off her face with the tail of her dress, then inched out the door and along the back of the barn to the side opposite the corral. The bucket bumped against the barn, and she stopped dead still. The sound seemed to go on forever. Had anyone else heard it? No one came to check on the noise, so she kept walking. She stopped at the corner of the barn and looked at the windmill. She had several feet of open space to cover. Could she do it? Or should she forget the water and run back to the safety of the barn?

She stiffened her spine. She would get water! She glanced around to make sure no one was looking toward the windmill, then, with her heart in her mouth, dashed to the tank and held the bucket under the spout. It seemed to take forever for the water even to half fill the bucket. At last she lifted it back away from the spout and carried it across the open space to the shelter of the barn. Her heart beat so hard, she was sure everyone at the whole farm could hear it.

She slipped into the barn, listened, and ran to the ladder that led up into the haymow. Before she could start up, she heard voices outside the barn. She ducked behind the barrels and peeked out. Her heart stopped. Splashes of water made a trail right to the barrels!

13
Rann

Trembling, Sadie set the bucket beside her as she hid behind the barrels. She wanted to toss dirt over the splashes of water, but there wasn't time. Whoever was coming was almost at the door. She waited, her knees knocking.

Muttering angrily, Stout walked in and right to the door to the tack room. The scar across his jutting chin seemed to show up even more than before. He smelled like sweat and looked as if he hadn't taken a bath in years.

Sadie held her breath so he wouldn't hear a sound from her. He hadn't seen the water splashes, but soon he'd see an empty room! What would she do then?

He slid back the bolt, and the sound seemed to echo forever inside the barn.

Sadie willed the girls in the haymow to sit quietly without making a peep.

Stout pushed the door in. "Mr. Wippet wants you . . ." His voice trailed off, and then he stuck his head into the room with his hands hanging tightly onto the doorjamb. He looked around as if he thought the girls were hiding behind the harness or under a saddle. Finally he spun around with a mighty roar and raced out into the yard, shouting, "They're gone! Them girls are gone!"

Sadie grabbed the water bucket and scrambled up into the haymow. Quickly she told the girls what had happened while they took turns drinking. Even as she talked she knew she had to figure a way to send Wippet on a false trail. A killdeer will pretend to have a broken wing as it half hops and half flies away from its nest on the ground to lead an enemy away. Sadie frowned. What could *she* do? Just then she glanced at Opal as she drank from the bucket. Her ribbon dangled down from her tangled dark hair. Sadie snatched it off Opal's head and looked for something heavy to wrap it around. She spotted a short square-headed nail and quickly wrapped the ribbon around it, warning the girls not even to whisper. She ran lightly to the back window of the haymow and pitched the nail and ribbon out as far as she could. The ribbon came untangled and floated to the grass while the nail kept going. The ribbon made a splash of color in the fresh green grass. It would be very easy to see. If anyone found the ribbon, they'd assume the girls had run in that direction.

Sadie started back across the haymow when loud voices filled the barn below. She stopped in her tracks. She didn't dare move or she'd send dust and hay particles floating down through the cracks. Her mouth felt bone-dry, and her tongue clung to the roof of her mouth.

"Look over every part of this barn!" Wippet shouted.

Sadie shivered. The girls clamped their hands over their mouths to hold back screams of fear.

From outside the back of the barn someone shouted, "I found a ribbon! It belongs to that girl . . . Opal!"

Everyone rushed out of the barn, and the girls breathed easier.

Sadie walked softly across to the water bucket and drank. The water felt cold and wet against her lips and mouth and throat. Finally she set the bucket down, picked up the rifle, and walked to the front window to peer out.

Just then Rann rode Soot out of the corral and across the yard. Someone shouted, and a shot rang out. Soot reared, but Rann stayed on his back.

Sadie pressed her hand to her racing heart as she and the girls watched Rann try to get Soot under control so he could ride him out into the prairie to freedom. The others swarmed back to the yard to watch, but stayed far back to keep from being kicked by the wild-eyed black horse.

Rann leaned low in the saddle and spoke to Soot and finally calmed him. Without looking back at the crowd behind him, Rann nudged him toward the prairie. Soot shot forward just as Stout leaped at him. Stout caught the bridle strap and jerked, then lost his hold and fell to the ground. His eyes wild, Soot screamed again from the pain the bit caused, shook his head, then reared high. Rann grabbed the saddle horn and held on tight. Soot bucked like a bucking bronco at a rodeo. Each landing jarred Rann until he thought his bones would break.

Suddenly Rann lost his hold, sailed out of the saddle, and landed hard on the sandy ground.

Sadie gasped. Rann had failed again!

Soot snorted and kicked, then ran off into the prairie, the reins flipping around his front legs.

Rann groaned and slowly pushed himself up to his knees. He wanted to bury himself in the sand and never face the agony he knew was coming. Wippet would probably kill him on the spot. For sure he'd beat him with his whip.

Sadie watched Rann with tears in her eyes. Poor Rann! He'd wanted his freedom so desperately.

"We must help him," Opal whispered brokenly.

"Yes." Sadie nodded, and the Elston sisters agreed. But what could they do?

In the yard Horace Wippet strode over to Rann, grabbed him by the hair, and hauled him to his feet. "You are dead, boy!"

Rann struggled a while, but Wippet held him tightly by his hair. Wippet's face turned brick-red as he ranted and raved. Finally Rann stopped struggling and stood with his shoulders bent and his head down. Wippet's voice was hoarse from yelling.

Sadie could barely breathe as she watched the scene below. Silence fell over the yard, with Wippet's angry tirade the only sound. With a smirk on his face, Stout stood to the side. Book covered her face with her hands as Tiffin stepped closer to her. The other guards stood ready to act at Wippet's command.

Finally Wippet stopped shouting. The great silence stretched on and on and on. Wippet angrily raised his whip to strike Rann.

Sadie suddenly knew what she had to do. She snapped the rifle to her shoulder, took careful aim, and fired—almost all in the same instant. The bullet struck the whip handle and splintered it. It flew from Wippet's hand even as he staggered back. He tried to catch his balance, lost his hold on Rann, and fell to the ground.

Rann leaped to his feet and raced for the barn. Stout started after him. Sadie shot the ground in front of the man's feet, and he stopped short, giving Rann enough time to reach the barn.

One of the guards shot toward the haymow. Sadie dropped to her stomach and shot down at the guard. She hit his hat right where she'd aimed and sent it sailing. He cried out and ran for cover behind the house. The other guards followed.

Sadie looked at the girls and smiled. They still weren't out of danger, but it was a beginning. Only she knew that the only ammunition she had to hold the guards at bay was what was loaded in the rifle, and that wouldn't last much longer.

Rann reached the haymow and dropped down beside Sadie. "Thanks."

She smiled.

Just then from down below someone started to sing "Count Your Blessings."

Sadie laughed right out loud and joined in, as did Opal and the Elston girls.

The song rang out into the prairie and curled around the hills.

Wippet stood up with his arms in the air and screamed at the top of his lungs. He looked ready to burst. He ran at the crowd, but they stood their ground and sang louder.

Sadie caught Opal's hand and squeezed hard.

14
Freedom

Caleb lifted his head and listened. Was that singing he heard over the noise of the wagon? He pulled back on the reins and listened. It *was* singing! Had they been wrong about The Poor Farm? He glanced at Indigo beside him and knew he wasn't. She'd caught them just as they were leaving town and had begged to ride along. Wilson had wanted her to stay in town so she'd be out of danger, but Caleb had let her ride with him because he could tell she was set on going back to the farm—whether with them or on her own. Wilson rode nearby with Scott Elston and Mike Treet beside him. Caleb waved the men on ahead just as they'd planned so they could surround the area. He urged the team forward and soon drove into sight of The Poor Farm. He frowned as he watched Wippet running wildly back and forth in front of the singing crowd. Four men stood at the side of the house, their guns pointed at the big barn.

Caleb grinned at Indigo. This was not what he'd expected. "You say you gave your rifle to Sadie Rose?"

"Yes." Indigo locked her hands in her lap, frightened at the scene before her. "Can she use it?"

"Sure can. She can shoot the croak out of a frog without harming one hair on it."

Indigo laughed. "That's good shooting."

"That's my Sadie Rose." Caleb swelled with pride as he rode right on into the yard and stopped beside Wippet.

Wilson, Scott, and Mike disarmed the guards and walked them into the yard to join the party.

Wippet waved his hands as if to shoo Caleb away. "Get off my property!" Wippet stamped his foot like a spoiled child.

"You'll be the one that's leaving," Caleb said softly.

Indigo dropped down beside Wippet and jabbed her finger at him. "The whole town will know your secret."

Wippet started to swear, and Wilson cuffed him hard across the face. The deposed king sank to the ground with his head down and his shoulders bent in defeat.

"Sadie Rose!" Caleb shouted as he leapt to the ground.

She jumped up in the haymow doorway. "Here, Daddy!"

Opal joined Sadie and waved high. "We knew you'd come back!"

Victoria and Clarissa stuck their heads around Sadie and Opal. "Pa!" they called in relief.

Scott waved and raced for the barn.

As the Elston girls scrambled down the ladder, Sadie turned around and found Rann with tears streaming down his face. "What's wrong? You're finally free!"

He brushed at his tears, but they kept right on falling. "I tried so long to get away and then gave up. I'm sure glad you girls came along!"

Sadie and Opal looked at each other and shook their heads. In a way they weren't glad they'd come along. It had been the worst time they'd ever had in their whole lives. Sadie finally said, "Being here has been terrible, but we're glad we could help set you and the others free."

Just outside the barn Scott hugged his girls as if he would never let them go again. "Your ma has been worried," he said hoarsely.

"We missed her," Clarissa said.

"We missed you too, Pa." Victoria kissed his cheek, then flushed. She hadn't kissed him since she'd turned five. After this, she'd kiss him on a regular basis. Ma too.

Inside the barn Sadie dropped from the ladder and right into Caleb's strong arms. She hugged him as tightly as she could. He smelled like sweat and leather, same as usual. He hugged her so hard, she thought her ribs would crack.

Opal dropped down, expecting to land on the dirt floor, but instead landed in Michael Treet's arms. She flushed and tried to push away.

"I'm glad you're safe," he whispered brokenly, his blue eyes sparkling with unshed tears.

Her heart skipped a beat, and she managed to smile. "Put me down, please." Was that all she could ever say to him?

"I will." But he held her until Caleb released Sadie and turned to hug Opal.

119

Sadie stepped to Rann's side as he stood there watching the happy reunion. "I'd like to see your family when you finally get home."

Rann shivered. "Maybe they forgot me."

"How could they? You're their son."

Rann shrugged and tried to believe what Sadie said. Just then Soot trotted into the barn and walked right up to Rann.

Caleb had heard what Sadie and Rann had said. "Suppose you bring your horse—he sure does act like your horse—and go back to town with us. We'll get you cleaned up so your folks will know you, and then we'll ride home with you."

Rann couldn't speak around the lump in his throat, but he nodded.

A few minutes later Sadie walked beside Caleb and Opal out into the yard. Wilson and Indigo were talking with the people one at a time to see who belonged there and who didn't. The others waiting to talk to Wilson and Indigo chattered with each other as if a dam of words had burst inside them.

Michael Treet listened for several minutes, then stepped forward. He called for silence. "I'll make sure these folks who don't belong here at the farm get paid for work they did and get back to their families."

As a cheer went up for Mike, Opal looked at him as if he were the most wonderful man in the whole world.

Sadie frowned at Opal and whispered for her ears alone, "You're forgetting all about Ellis Hepford again."

Opal smiled dreamily. "Mike is grand." Then she became very businesslike. "Besides, I won't see Mike after tomorrow."

Just then Tiffin stepped up to Caleb and introduced himself. "I worked for Wippet, but I never did kill nobody. Me and Book here plan on getting married, and we thought maybe we could be in charge of The Poor Farm from now on. I know how to run the glove factory and the rest of the place too. I can understand if you don't trust me, but we both turned over a new leaf. Honest."

Caleb saw the sincerity in Tiffin's eyes. "You'll have to talk to the townsfolk. Indigo told me how you let her go, and that says a lot for you. You can talk to her and Mike about what you want to do. They could put in a good word to the town fathers for you."

"Thank you," Book said softly. This time the book peeking out of her apron pocket was a Bible.

The next morning Sadie sat on one side of Caleb and Opal on the other as they headed for Rann's place. He rode Soot beside the wagon. Sadie looked at Rann and shook her head. He didn't look like the same boy. His hair was cut and combed neatly, he was clean, and he wore a pair of Levis, a plaid shirt, and cowboy boots along with a wide-brimmed hat. Caleb had helped him choose his clothes, and he'd paid for them with money Tiffin had given him from the cash in Wippet's safe.

Opal glanced over her shoulder even though she knew Starr was hidden behind several hills. She'd said a long, tender good-bye to Mike, thankful she wouldn't have to choose between Mike and El. Starr was too far away from the Circle Y for Mike to ever come calling. But it was easier that way. It was hard to choose which fine young man she really wanted to marry.

Caleb smiled, glad to be heading for home with only a stop at Rann's family home. Wilson and Indigo were going to ride with wagon loads of lumber leaving the lumberyard tomorrow for the Circle Y. They were making plans to get married before they left Starr.

Caleb glanced back at the load of lumber he was bringing with him. Between that lumber and the lumber Wilson and Indigo were bringing later, Bess would soon have her frame house. Caleb's heart leapt at the thought of seeing Bess. She'd be worried that they weren't back in time, but he'd wipe away the worry with a kiss.

An hour later Sadie locked her hands in her lap as Caleb drove past a barn and a windmill and stopped in the yard outside a small frame house. Chickens scratched in the yard. A donkey lifted its head and brayed. Sadie glanced at Rann. He'd stopped Soot beside the wagon, but he stayed in the saddle. She knew he was scared.

Finally the screen door opened, and a woman with two small children stepped out. She looked tired and sad.

Sadie, Caleb, and Opal waited for Rann to speak. Finally he slipped off Soot and stepped toward the woman. Trembling, he pulled off his hat and studied the woman before him. She looked like his ma, yet she didn't. He was as tall as she was! Could three years make that much difference?

"Could I help you?" the woman asked, looking intently at Rann.

He cleared his throat. "Ma? It's me . . . Rann."

She gasped and clutched at her throat. "Don't go pulling no jokes on me, boy. My son Rann is . . . gone."

Sadie locked her hands in her lap. She felt the tension in the air and silently prayed for Rann and his ma.

Rann shook his head. "No, Ma. I'm here. I know

your name is Lil, and your husband is Conner
Mathis. I'm Rann. You named me after Pa's grand-
dad back in Virginia. These young 'uns are Bart and
Meg."

Lil's eyes filled with tears and she shook her
head. "Rann?"

"Yes, Ma."

She caught his hands and squeezed them, then
with a cry flung her arms around him and held him
tight.

He held her as if he'd never let her go. Finally he
stepped back from her. "Where's Pa?"

"With Lee on the spring roundup." She dried her
eyes with her apron tail. "They won't be back for a
couple of days."

"I could go help them."

"No!" Lil gripped his hand. "I don't want you out
of my sight for a good long time!"

Rann smiled, glad to hear the love in her voice.
He glanced up at Sadie, and she was smiling and
brushing tears from her eyes. "Ma, I want you to
meet some real good people." He introduced her to
the Yorks in a voice full of pride.

Caleb tipped his hat. "It's a pleasure to meet
you, ma'am."

"Please stay for a bit and eat with us," Lil said.

"We'd sure like to, but we've got to get ourselves
and this load of lumber home."

Sadie wanted to get home too, but she'd have
liked to stay to see Rann's pa when he got home and
found his long-lost son there.

Rann reached up for Sadie's hand. She held it
down to him, and they clasped hands and smiled.

"Be sure to visit the Circle Y when you can," she
said.

"I will. I promise." Rann clamped his hat on his

little brother's head and caught his little sister's hand. "My whole family will come."

Sadie smiled.

Caleb said his good-byes, then clucked to Dick and Jane. They stepped forward, and the wagon moved with a jerk.

Sadie watched the prairie grass rippling in the constant Nebraska wind as they headed for home. She looked back and waved again at Rann and his family standing in the yard, then looked ahead. Soon Momma would have her frame house. Soon the prisoners from The Poor Farm would be back with their families.

Sadie peeked around Caleb at Opal and sang, "Count your blessings, name them one by one . . ." Opal joined in, and so did Caleb.

Pushing her bonnet off, Sadie tipped back her head and sang with tears in her eyes. She had so many blessings, she couldn't count them all. She and Opal were alive and well and on their way home, and God would be with them always, no matter what!